The Sheikh Bear

Ashley Hunter

Copyright 2015 by Ashley Hunter

All rights reserved.
No part of this publication may be reproduced in any way whatsoever, without written permission from the author, except in case of brief quotations embodied in critical reviews and articles.

This is a work of fiction. Any resemblance to any person, living or dead, is purely coincidental.
First edition, 2015

Chapter 1

Elle Roberts wasn't what you'd call a supremely confident woman. Granted, she was comfortable with her looks, she was comfortable with herself—but she wasn't exactly the type to put herself *out* there.

She lived her life in a small town growing up. The same people during elementary school became the people she knew throughout high school. She had one boyfriend, a sweet guy who loved art more than anything; it just took her some time to realize that the list that included 'anything' also included her. So when he told her he was going to a college far off to pursue his dream as an artist, she was broken hearted when he said he'd be going alone.

Still, she didn't want to appear pushy or clingy and so when he broke it off, Elle smiled, gave him a warm hug, and wished him luck. Not long after he left did she finally decide to leave that small town herself.

There were too many eyes that knew about her relationship, too many people who talked about how it was 'such a shame' and 'they looked so cute together.' So when her Uncle offered her a place to stay in the city, Elle sort of made a mad-dash decision and left.

If one could die from culture shock, Elle would have been six feet under after her first couple of weeks within that concrete jungle. People went about their business without caring about her, cars and taxis zoomed back and forth in an endless chase of clients and destinations and the only thing that Elle could truly register after a few nights of restless sleep; the city was *loud.*

"Are you sure you wouldn't like to come home?"

Her mother had asked her one late night after Elle had called, eyes clogged with tears and nose raw from wiping with tissues.

"I was talking to Maria, she said that Alex would be visiting in the fall."

Alex... The name alone made Elle's chest ache but she was already shaking her head at the idea.

"I'm staying, mom. I don't want to see him."

"I don't like the idea of you being out there on your own, even if your Uncle said you'd be taken care of in that penthouse. It's dangerous."

"Yeah, but…" Elle had said before she peered out the window of her new bedroom.

The lights below were astounding, as if she had been launched into space to live among a galaxy of stars.

"I like it here. I'll be fine."

"I'll be fine…"

The words sounded somewhat droll now that Elle found herself in a large and very expensive looking lobby. Everything about the place looked immaculate, down to the marble tile, the rugs, and the furniture placed exquisitely all around. Elle had never felt so out of place in all her life.

Her cousin, one of her Uncle's daughters, had recommended her to work there after they helped her update her resume.

Carla had pursed her lips at the document, blue eyes skimming Elle's life work before smiling and giving her a nod.

"You've got quite a lot of experience, cousin." Carla had said and Elle had beamed up at her happily.

"I'm sure you'll be able to fit in nicely."

Sure enough, just a week later (after a month in the city), Elle found herself in her best interview attire in one of the most high-class places she had ever seen.

The woman sitting in the reception desk had eyed her up and down once before directing her to a seat and with a professional smile that consisted of nearly blinding white teeth, told Elle to wait to be called on.

She had been waiting for nearly fifteen minutes and could feel her nerves continue to bite and chew and gnaw at her stomach. Glancing down at herself, Elle frowned. This was the best skirt she had, but it was old and it had a couple of stains on it that had been hard to remove.

Even her shirt and jacket, while she had believed were stylish, looked drab compared to the outfit worn by the woman in reception—and to her growing mortification—the other women and men that walked in and out of the lobby.

They all looked like models. Fresh off the cover of some fashion magazine!

And yet there she was, sitting in ill-fitted clothing, several sizes bigger than the toothpick-slim women walking around, and with her mess of wild brown curls pinned down to a half-knot in the back of her head.

Fifteen minutes became twenty and Elle snuck a glance at the nearest clock.

What was taking so long? Was she being tested? Was she being watched right now?

"Just be yourself, okay?" Carla had informed her earlier that week.

"It's a secretary position and so you'll be expected to behave naturally. Your employer is actually one of our biggest clients, but don't feel pressured, he's really not that bad."

"He sounds like a big deal…" Elle had laughed nervously.

"He's a Sheikh from Dubai, and the guy is really well off. His family's business has been in

liaison with ours for a long time, so I have no doubt that you'll do well."

"Elle Roberts?"

Elle shot off from her seat, more out of alarm than intention and when she searched for the source of the voice she was suddenly under the sharp scrutiny of an extremely well dressed silver-blonde woman.

This woman was all angles and impressionable colors. A blouse of deep vermilion swathed over her pale skin and shimmered beneath the light of the chandeliers above. Black pencil skirt hugged her legs and enhanced her features and no doubt those were 'chimmy choos' (or whatever they were called) gracing her feet. Elle felt so ridiculously underdressed.

The woman noticed. With a pointed look at her skirt, the woman fixed her an unimpressed glare before turning with her chin.

"This way."

Elle followed quickly, nearly stumbling over her heels as she struggled to catch up to the woman's strut.

"We've looked over your resume," the woman spoke without warning.

"Oh! Uh…"

"Impressive work, considering. Of course, we did expect someone… different. Your credentials are more than enough to get you hired." The woman said, never slowing down her pace as she led Elle down a hallway that was just crawling with unbelievably good-looking people.

"Now, the Sheikh will be waiting for you to assist in a few small errands, more to gauge how much you can take at once. He'll be expecting his coffee as well as his first 'rules' of the day. You'll be speaking with Avani—the Sheikh's first secretary and she'll be giving you a rundown as well as your training of what you need to do, so save your questions for her."

"You should know that while you are here, you need to maintain a certain standard of appearance," she said this as she shot Elle a look of thinly veiled disdain.

"The Sheikh is a very important figure in business and his secretary should look the part."

"Oh, of course…" Elle muttered, cheeks burning.

"I'll have you know that you're not the first woman who's walked in here expecting a simple job. The Sheikh's already fired his five previous secretaries, after Avani, of course."

Elle blinked curiously as they took another turn down a hallway.

"Wait… what happened to Avani?"

"Ugh, she went and got herself married and now she's pregnant." The woman sighed as though the whole situation was a huge inconvenience.

Elle was nearly baffled at the reaction.

"Which was a huge deal considering since the Sheikh has been giving all other women a hard time. But he's absolutely gorgeous so you should count your lucky stars or something."

"Uh…" Elle was at a loss for words.

"Sorry, I never got your name?"

"Alliana." The woman said, "But you won't need to remember it, since we'll probably never see each other again. Here we are."

She paused for a moment after they arrived to a long set of double doors of a deep mahogany.

"Avani is inside and waiting for you, so do as your told and maybe you'll be lucky. Ta'."

And just like that Alliana was sauntering off, expensive heels clacking away. Elle watched her disappear down a hallway before glancing back at the door.

With a sigh, she leaned over and lifted a hand to knock before she changed her mind and grasped the fine sterling handle.

With a turn and push, Elle made her way inside the room and nearly gasped when she beheld her surroundings. The office was beautifully done and since it was near the top of the building, immense glass windows became the walls near the far end.

The view outside was spectacular, and the light of the day glanced off from the surrounding buildings made it look all the more enchanting. Before Elle could find herself entranced, her green eyes managed to fall over the only person sitting in the suite.

Elle had been told she would meet Avani, but the figure lying on the white couch adjacent to the windows was certainly not Avani, but a very well dressed man.

He was covered in a fine suit of a beautiful shade of cream and burgundy trim. He had an arm over his eyes so Elle couldn't see his face clearly, but he looked to be at ease. Long legs resting over the white cushions, and his broad chest was moving gently, he looked like he was napping.

Elle took in a cautionary breath, uncertain on what to do. Her first instinct was to turn around and leave, cursing herself for not having knocked earlier.

To her surprise, Elle wasn't given an opportunity.

"Are you going to just stand there all day or are you going to come here?" The man spoke, not moving an inch aside from speaking. His voice was an attractive baritone with a lilt to his words that reminded Elle of a British accent, yet he rolled his tongue over some of the words pleasantly.

Elle was spurred forward, taking a few steps deeper into the suite before she was standing a respectful distance from the couch.

Finally, he lifted his arm from his eyes, thick brows arching as he beheld her.

"And you are?"

"Elle Roberts…?" Elle began, trying not to squirm visibly.

"I'm starting as the new secretary for the Sheikh Zayn Ab…Ab…"

"Zayn Abd al Malik," he replied, his tongue rolling over the name with almost lazy precision.

"Starting as his secretary and you can't even say your employer's name?"

Elle flushed pink, "I'll be sure to say it properly when I meet him."

"I'm sure," he drawled, settling over the cushions as he watched her, bored.

"Did Alliana bring you here?"

"Yes," Elle replied. "She said I would meet with Avani?"

"Avani's water broke," he replied with a half shrug.

"She should be delivering her brat sometime within the next hour or so…"

Elle swallowed, unsure how to register this man's abrupt bitter tone.

"I see…"

"So, guess that means you'll have no one to train you. Which sucks—as you people love to say—since the Sheikh is a serious hardass." The man pushed himself up to sit and face her.

"You know the Sheikh?" Elle asked curiously.

She felt strangely hot now that she was speaking to this man. He was unbelievably attractive. Dark skin and dark hair that curled in messy waves over his scalp and teased his dark eyes.

"You could say that," he replied, smirking.

"Although, I doubt you want to know him, dressed like that." He added, waving a finger in her direction in a loose gesture.

Elle glanced down at her clothes, lip sinking behind her teeth. "If he saw you like that, *habibi*, he'd rip you apart."

A bubble of irritation set her nerves on fire.

Elle glanced back up at the man with a scowl, "I didn't come here to play dress up, I came here to work, mister…?" She trailed off.

"Malik." He said, smirk widening. Elle blinked in surprise.

"You're related to the Sheikh?"

"In a matter of speaking," he said with a snicker.

"Since you're so eager to work, maybe I should put you to it. Trial by fire, or so they say right, *habibi*?"

Suddenly, he was up on his feet, heading towards a door at the other side of the suite. "I'm certain you know all about the Rules, know how the Sheikh loves to take his coffee. Also, you know all about the Schedule, right?"

"The—what?" Elle stammered, unsure whether to follow him or not.

"Wonderful! The Sheikh is a stickler for the schedule, and if you don't have that memorized like it's your mother's name then you won't last long." He said and continued to say after he walked through the door that lead to a fairly large office space.

Elle finally decided to go after him.

"I won't need to show you to your desk since you probably already know where it is, so you better hop to it!"

The office was pretty immense, two desks sat in opposite sides of the room facing each other. The room continued into another room with glass doors, where one could see an immense desk and several other assortments needed for a business.

Malik strolled in through the room before whirling around and facing her. Elle nearly collided into him, stopping short to take several steps away from his dark stare.

"Are you fond of challenges, Miss Roberts?"

"Uh—Y-yes?"

"Good, because this one is probably one you're not suited for. The past five girls that came here hardly lasted a couple of weeks—although one of them managed to get a full month in before she was fired."

"All of them had impressive credentials and all of them were much better dressed than you. You're out of your league here, Miss Roberts. So, I'd recommend you turn around and go home before making any other decisions."

Elle frowned, squaring her shoulders. She had grown up in a comfortable small town and in a place where everyone knew each other, but she was a hard worker, and she was unmatched in organizing events and dealing with rough customers. She would not be cowed by some guy in an Armani suit.

"With all due respect, Mr. Malik, I appreciate your warning, but I didn't come all this way to give up. I may not look like the women out there, but I've got something none of them have."

Malik rose a brow, "Oh, and what's that?"

Elle fixed him a defiant stare.

"Determination. So you can go tell the Sheikh that I'm not going to get beaten that easily."

Malik let out a low laugh before grinning at her, "I'll be sure to let him know. Good luck, *habibi*. You're going to need it."

And with that he turned and walked out of the office suite, leaving Elle on her own.

When Elle returned to her uncle's apartment late that night, it had been the first time she had broken down into a fit of tears that had nothing to do with Alex.

Chapter 2

The next day, Elle walked into the building dressed in her battle armor—a business tracksuit that her mother had purchased for her years ago that she had never bothered wearing. She had no doubt that the outfit was out of style, but Elle wasn't about to show up again to be shown up by some high-fashioned idiots.

She had styled her hair differently this time as well, her wild mane of curls now sat behind her head in a messy bun that she accentuated with a flowery hair clip. Her eyes and face had a little more serious make up and when she appeared toward the reception desk, the woman sitting there seemed to ignore her easily rather than stare at her pointedly. This was some progress, Elle supposed, but she wasn't finished yet.

She headed up towards the office, prepared to follow the steps of her work like she had been told. The training of yesterday was a disaster. She had gotten the coffee wrong, had mixed up some of the documents for a meeting, and nearly missed an important call from one of the Sheikh's clients.

In all that time, she had never met her employer and Malik had only shown up once to laugh at her when she was busy scrambling for the right documents to take to the meeting.

"I'm surprised he isn't firing you, *habibi*. Women have been fired for less." He had said with a devious grin.

"Well, maybe if you didn't just stand there and helped me, I wouldn't have my neck on the chopping block." Elle snapped back, already tired of this man's hovering.

"Be careful, *habibi*."

He clicked his tongue at her, "You don't want to get thrown out because of your attitude, do you?"

Elle sighed before stamping down her frustration and getting back to work.

Eventually, the end of the workday came and Elle still hadn't met the Sheikh.

Now that she was marching up, she made a turn before nearly running into Alliana. The woman was dressed in magnificent colors of gold and emerald and Elle barely had enough time to gawk at her wardrobe before her guide was glaring her at.

"You're late." Alliana stated.

Elle blinked in surprise before glancing down at her wristwatch—a gift from her uncle—and the time was a few minutes before she was due to be at her desk.

"I thought my schedule is from nine to five?"

Alliana let out a low noise of disgust.

"And what you think the Sheikh is going to get his own morning coffee, or make sure his dry cleaning is on time? No. That's your job and you're late."

Elle fought the urge to let out a wail before she was suddenly being whisked away by the blonde woman.

"Since apparently you're still new and Avani is unable to train you, I suppose I have to show you how it's done before you ruin everything."

The following few hours were spent with Elle being drilled on coffee temperatures, times and directions for the dry cleaning, restaurants the Sheikh preferred to eat from and what meals to avoid.

She was then informed on the Schedule—an immense spreadsheet that was comprised online and on her computer. Using her phone, Elle would receive notifications for each upcoming event, and make sure the Sheikh was informed of every change, be it infinitely tiny or otherwise.

Her office phone led to several places and she was drilled on which speed dials led her where. Alliana had even slapped her wrist when Elle had nearly dialed a wrong number. It was mortifying.

However, Malik was nowhere to be seen and so that was some relief. She didn't know how she would react to having that man laughing at her for being scolded like a child.

Finally, Alliana brought Elle a large binder before nearly slamming it on the desk. Elle jumped at the sound, before turning a meek glance to the severe looking woman.

"These, Elle, are the Rules. You memorize them, you breathe them, you become them. You do not break the rules, you do not bend the rules. You make sure all of these are followed to the very letter or you will be packing up your things and being sent out of here faster than you can even care to say your own name. Make sure you've got everything down, because if I hear just one complaint from the Sheikh, I will *not* be happy."

Elle nodded quickly, swallowing thickly as she looked down at the binder.

Gingerly, she opened the cover before looking down at the page. She nearly blanched when her eyes fell over one of the rules.

"Alliana, what does it mean that I must attend to the Sheikh's every needs?"

The woman let out a noise that sounded like an incredulous laugh.

"I'm sure I don't need to explain it, Elle. You're a smart woman, you can figure it out. Now, will that be all your questions or do I need to spell everything out for you? I have important matters to attend to."

Elle shook her head quietly before turning the page. Allianna gave her a short nod.

"Good. Don't screw up."

And with that, she sauntered off not unlike how she did the other day.

Alone, Elle peered over the rules and pondered over them. Some of these were absolutely ridiculous. *Never speak to the Sheikh directly unless spoken to. Never look at the Sheikh unless permitted.*

It was as if she was working for an alien rather than a human being. Still, he came from a far off place and one that Elle had never really heard of aside from her world's geography class back in high school.

"Having trouble?" Elle heard and she nearly jumped out of her skin.

Turning around, she saw Malik leaning against the doorframe, smirking at her with amusement. He was dressed in a dark violet three-piece suit, perfectly tailored to his broad and slim figure.

"No…" Elle said, frowning.

"I'm just looking over the rules. Some of these are a bit extreme."

"Oh?" Malik asked, "Thinking about quitting?"

Elle fixed the dark skinned man a flat stare before turning back to her work.

"It's just some of these are sort of vague. Like… I have to make sure the Sheikh's needs are all attended? What does that mean?"

Suddenly she felt Malik right behind her. His abrupt presence made her skin shiver and feel tight, and when she glanced up, he was grinning down at her wickedly.

"What do you think it means, Miss Roberts?"

Elle fought the urge to push away, feeling disturbed by this man's nerve.

"I think it means that the Sheikh really needs a mother, not a secretary."

Malik pushed away, letting out a short laugh before placing his hands in his pockets.

"Don't let him hear you say that. Otherwise it'll be the can for you."

"Then I'm glad he's not around," Elle replied, taking a breath to calm her down. The comment brought up a question she had been meaning to ask.

"Speaking of which, where *is* the Sheikh? I haven't met him since I've arrived even though

I've been sending all the information and placing his coffee in his office."

"He's a lot closer than you think, *habibi*." Malik said before heading towards the empty desk feet away from her.

He leaned against the edge, watching her with unreadable eyes.

"What is that? That word you keep calling me?" Elle asked, thumbing over the pages of the Rules before shutting them close.

"It's a term we have for dear, *habibi*" Malik explained.

"Nothing insulting. So no need to fret. If anything, it's an endearing term."

"I'm sure," Elle said, before turning back to her work.

"Anyway, I hope you don't mind if I just continue working…"

"Why would I mind?" Malik inquired, looking rather comfortable watching her. Elle fought the urge to kick him out, but was still wary about where he came from.

In all honesty, she didn't know him, just that he was somehow related to the Sheikh and that he clearly had the permission to move about as he pleased.

"Can I ask you something?"

Malik blinked, dark eyes narrowing somewhat before he gave her a sudden grin, "If you want to know where the nearest exit is, it's in the back."

Elle felt a twitch begin in the arch of her eyebrow.

"That's not what I want to ask. You said you're related to the Sheikh, right?"

"In a matter of speaking," he replied as vaguely as he did the day before.

"What's he like?" The question seemed to surprise Malik, because one moment he was smiling at her, the next a strange emotion passed over his face.

It disappeared much too quickly for Elle to tell what it was before he let out a small scoff of amusement and pushing away from the desk.

"You better worry more about yourself than that guy, Miss Roberts. Trust me, he's out of your league."

A red flush burned up and over Elle's neck and into her face, making her steam with irritation.

"That's not why I was asking, Mister Malik!" But he was already slinking away, his steps languid and graceful before he disappeared out the door with a final wave.

Elle glared at the direction Malik disappeared off to before getting back to work. That evening when she returned, Elle was exhausted and was sporting several papercuts over her fingers, but it had gone better than it did her first day.

If there was anything she didn't want to do, it was running back home with her tail between her legs.

Chapter 3

She arrived the next morning an hour early, her phone ringing in her palm incessantly since she woke. Alliana's voice was shrill on the other side of the speaker, listing off a long list of orders Elle had barely managed to catch before hanging up and leaving the half-awake brunette spinning to get ready.

When she arrived, she had to jog back and forth between offices to deliver documents, pass out spreadsheets, and ensure members met memos before she was scrambling back towards the kitchenette where the Sheikh's coffee was being made.

By the time Elle made it next to the biggest espresso machine she had ever seen, she felt completely worn out.

"You're the new girl, aren't you?"

Elle straightened from her position next to the immense coffee maker, sleep drawing lines of inattention through her vision as she focused on the person speaking to her.

When she finally turned around, she saw a woman—who looked like she should still be in high school—leaning against the doorframe.

The posture reminded Elle far too quickly of a certain dark-skinned man and felt her stomach sour at the thought. She didn't know Malik enough, but of what she did know, she wasn't fond of it.

Shoving the bitterness in her stomach aside, Elle faced the woman directly.

"Uh, yes. I'm Elle. Elle Roberts."

"Charmed." The woman—girl?—said.

She was beautiful; with dark mocha colored skin and huge hazel eyes, her petite figure was wrapped in what looked like a Sari (a garb from India that Elle had been forced to recognize since the document debacle of her first day) but split away to show a pair of pale cream pants.

Her dark hair curled around her heart shaped face in ringlets and if it wasn't for the pointed look aimed at Elle, she would be a little endeared toward the girl.

"How've you been faring?"

Her accent was practically the same as Malik's, sounding like a mix between British and Arabic, and for a moment Elle wondered if this girl was his sister.

"I've been alright," Elle replied modestly and with a smile.

"Still getting used to this place. It's amazing."

"Hm, unsurprising. You don't look like much," the girl said and Elle started to feel a little annoyed. Why did everyone treat her like this?

"But, I suppose you'll do."

"Sorry, but, who are you?"

Elle asked, nearly biting down her tongue when she caught the hint of attitude escape through her teeth. The girl didn't seem to notice.

"Priya Abdul al Hamik," She replied flippantly.

"I'm your employer's second cousin and advisor. I heard about you, can't say I'm impressed."

"It's a pleasure to meet you," Elle said, reeling but nonetheless holding back from embarrassing herself further.

"I'm sure it is," Priya replied.

"Anyway. Because Avani is indisposed for the next eternity, I've been assigned to supervise and train you. The last thing we need is you offending the Sheikh."

"I appreciate it," Elle said.

"I've memorized a good portion of the rules but I do have questions about some of them."

Priya rolled her eyes, "You and every other *gori*. Come. There is much to be done and you're late."

Elle nearly scrambled after the short Hindu woman, grabbing the coffee and the documents she was given earlier that morning.

When they reached the business suite, Priya had launched into a series of commands that had Elle feeling like she was in boot camp. She needed to straighten up, freshen up, send out new spreadsheets and call for a special broth that the Sheikh would need to begin his day.

The glass doors that lead to the Sheikh's office were closed and covered by a purple curtain on the other side. It was the first time Elle had seen this and felt a twinge of worry when she wondered if the Sheikh had finally decided to appear.

An hour later, Priya was looking over the Schedule in a tablet, her dainty fingers skimming over the glass screen swiftly.

"Hm." Priya finally let out, and Elle prepared herself for the next series of commands.

Instead, Priya was placing the tablet down before urging Elle to stand up. "Up. I want to see you."

Confused, Elle did as she was told spinning around awkwardly when Priya made circular motions with a finger.

"Not too bad," Priya muttered through pursed lips.

"Very well. We're leaving."

"Wait—what? Wh-where are we going?" Elle stammered, barely registering how quickly Priya was gathering her things and urging her out the door.

There were still a bunch of duties she needed to complete!

"Shopping, *gori*. While you may be comfortable sitting in those rags, while you're in the presence of the Sheikh, you will not be dressed like that."

Gawking, Elle followed numbly, nearly overwhelmed with surprise. "But, I don't have the money—!"

"Nuance." Priya shrugged off before yanking Elle out the door and taking her out on the strangest shopping trip of the young woman's life.

Chapter 4

"Ho, ho!" Malik's voice was absolutely gleeful. Embarrassment yanked its way through Elle's stomach, anchoring her to the ground almost painfully.

"Look at you, *habibi*. You look completely different! I almost mistook you for someone else!"

Shopping with Priya had been worse than anything Elle had gone through. They went through fittings and clothing stores so quickly, it left Elle's mind in a whirlwind and her feet aching.

When they finally concluded the purchase of clothes that Elle would probably never be able to purchase in a million years, they made their way to a salon where many of the staffs' women approached her like she had been beaten and bruised.

They sat her down, and began attacking her with all kinds of cosmetics and talked amongst one another in rapid Arabic.

Priya had been making commands since the start, and Elle had sat by—helpless—as they made their move and started filing her nails, rubbing oils over her skin, and tugging countless brushes over her wild hair.

When Elle managed to walk out the doors, her hair was soft and fell around her cheeks in lush waves and her face-felt heavy with make-up.

When they returned, Priya had given her a new list of things to memorize. Everything she needed to do and what clothes to match to make herself look presentable for the Sheikh.

To her utter despair, when Elle finally arrived back at the office to finish a few last minute things before heading home, Malik had been waiting next to her desk.

He glanced at her once before doing a double take, a huge Cheshire grin blooming over his face before he let out a chuckle.

"I dare say it, but you even look like the sort of woman that might tempt the Sheikh!" Malik exclaimed.

"Hilarious, Mister Malik."

Elle retorted, far too tired to do any better than that.

"I'm more impressed you survived Priya's fabulous make-over from hell," Malik continued.

"You know she's actually made women cry? Insanely strong women too, I'm surprised you're still here."

This man was on an entire new level of rude. Elle thought with clenched teeth.

Fed up, Elle finally turned to face him, "Is there anything else you'd like to say or can I go back to work now?"

"Yes. That blouse you're wearing?"

Malik pointed, "You might want to unbutton a couple of those, because your breasts look like they're choking."

"Get *out*!" Outrage burned through Elle's body and before she knew it, she was taking a few steps toward Malik before spinning him around and nearly shoved him out the door.

When she finally slammed the door shut, she heard a bark of laughter on the other side of the door.

Elle wanted to hide under her desk and die.

Chapter 5

"She did *what* now?" Priya exclaimed, cheeks burning hot with anger.

"You know your face does this hilarious thing when you're angry. Did you know that?"

"This isn't funny, Zayn!" The petite woman exclaimed before whirling around, dark ringlets flying about her head in a rage.

"I don't care if that *gori* has credentials from the bloody president!"

"Priya, take a deep breath." Zayn replied, rolling his eyes as he casually unfastened his tie from around his neck.

"You can't honestly expect a woman to not do that after a man points out the matters of her breasts, do you?"

The brunette scowled, crossing her arms over her chest stoutly.

"What I don't understand is why you are playing this idiot game with her? You're her employer and you let her throw you out of *your* office? You fired the last girl for mixing up your coffee, and you still want to keep this one around? If she had any idea who you are—"

"That's exactly why I want to keep her around, Priya." The Sheikh chuckled before turning around.

"Now that Avani's gone, don't you think I deserve a little fun?"

This was not well met by the woman, "I do not like this game, Zayn. I do not like you pretending to be some idiot pushing some *gori's* buttons for amusement. She's your secretary, and you're the heir to an important business empire. Act like it!"

A small silence fell between the two as Zayn moved toward the couch of the large business suite. When he settled on it, he found Priya's gaze to be piercing daggers into his skin.

Night time already fell over the building, and the brilliant lights of the city were the only thing next to a few dim lamps to cast some light over them. Even in the poor lighting, he could still see Priya's angry expression and was reminded of a time when they were children and she would glare at him just as hotly whenever he took one of her dolls and hid it.

"Are you acting like this because of Avani, Malik?" Priya asked, and while her voice had softened, the accusation behind it didn't.

The amusement in his chest sobered instantly to a dark expression. Zayn Abd al Malik remained silent even after he pulled a flask from within his breast pocket.

"Don't drink, answer the question." Priya insisted taking a few steps closer to yank the silver flask from her cousin's grip.

"Priya, let me be alone." Malik sighed.

"I will not leave you in peace until you answer me," she sat down next to him, leaning close to meet his gaze.

"If you're trying to entertain yourself because of a broken heart then fine, but go do that elsewhere. Not with this *gori* and certainly not wasting our time. We have matters to attend to and as Sheikh you need to start taking this seriously. The last thing I want is to tell father that you're playing stable boy with a silly white girl."

"What do you want me to do, Priya?" Malik asked, rubbing a palm over his face even after she stood and began to walk off.

"You want me to fire the girl? Because if that's what you want then I'll do it."

"No, Zayn. That is not what I want." Priya said before gazing at him somberly.

"I want you to work with her and do it properly. If you want to fire her, then let it be for a good reason. But I do not want you to be wasting your time acting out because the woman you loved picked another man and is now starting a family with him. You get up off your ass and you get to work. That is what you should do."

And without another word, Priya placed the flask on the end of the table between Malik and the door before she left. The young Sheikh listened as she disappeared and heaved out a heavy sigh.

Chapter 6

But that of course was easier said than done.

The following day when Zayn Abd al Malik arrived to the workplace, he was pleasantly surprised to find Elle asleep next to the coffee machine. It wasn't always you find a woman so amusing with her guard down.

As he approached, he noted that the espresso churning within the pot now brewing emitted a sweet aroma of vanilla and coconut. Such fragrances always made him want to sit and relax as well so it wasn't so unexpected that Elle would do so.

He almost felt sorry for her.

With a grin, he walked toward the small table where Elle was resting. Her hand cradled her jaw as her head drooped toward her chest. A thin stream of drool dribbled down the corner of her lip down to her chin. What an angel.

Cautiously, Malik pulled out the file on the table ahead of her. After a quick skim of the documents, Malik realized she was looking over one of the spreadsheets for the meeting at noon, and vaguely wondered what she was doing looking that over.

Closing the file, he was sorely tempted to take a picture of the dozing woman's face but knew that even doing that was pushing it.

Instead, he slapped the file over the wood with a loud '*whap!*'

Elle shot up, alarm flashing over her sleep-muddled green eyes as she let out a gasp. Malik stifled a snicker, settling instead on a smug smile that she caught the moment she looked up at him.

The way her expression flattened was almost just as satisfying as waking her up.

"Nice nap?"

The woman quickly countered hotly, "I was resting my eyes."

But the force of her statement fell apart when he patted a spot on his chin with a finger. She wiped the drool with the back of her hand, smudging her lipstick, much to her chagrin.

"Well, the Sheikh isn't paying you to rest your eyes." Malik replied chiefly, smile unwavering.

"By the way, aren't you late in delivering his coffee?"

"It's not like it matters." Elle replied, and the words actually surprised him.

"And why is that?"

She stretched in her seat and Malik couldn't help but notice the way her back arched and her body was accentuated prettily by the curve. It was honestly the first time since he saw her that he realized how pretty she was. Bizarre.

"Because he's never shown up to drink it. For all I know, the Sheikh's a ghost." The last word split into a yawn she covered behind a hand.

"Still, it's not exactly pay day either."

Malik took a few steps toward the counter to lean against it, inwardly amused at the fact that the very man Elle considered a ghost was standing right in front of her.

"Tsk, tsk, Miss Roberts. Better watch out for what you say, you wouldn't want the Sheikh to haunt you."

"I never believed in ghost stories, mister Malik." Elle replied, pulling out a high porcelain mug and coaster.

She proceeded to make the coffee without another glance at him and Malik watched her work, somewhat fascinated. It's only been five days since she had started and he couldn't find anything wrong with how she brewed his coffee.

This woman certainly had her head on her shoulders, he'd give her that. Still, it wasn't any fun seeing her behave so casually. He liked it better when she was frantic.

Yes, he was a bit of a sadist, but it wasn't always that he met someone so entertaining.

He could already hear Priya scolding him. Malik knew his play time was running out, so might as well make the best of it before he had to reveal himself. He had wanted to see how far he could keep up pretenses, but now it seemed that his little game was doomed to end quickly from the start.

"Give it here," Malik said as Elle began to walk off with coffee and file on hand. She paused to look at him curiously, her wild mane of curly hair subdued to pretty waves around her face.

He kind of liked her with the curls a little better, even if she did look prettier now. "I'll take it to the Sheikh."

To her credit, Elle refused to give him anything, "Not like I don't trust you or anything, mister Malik—"

"Please, just Malik. The whole mister thing sounds awful."

"—Fine. Malik. But, I would much rather take it myself." Elle tried to walk off ahead of him but he took a couple broad steps in front of her.

She gave him an annoyed stare this time—oh boy he couldn't wait to see the look on her face—before waiting for him to speak.

"I'm going to go see him right now, actually." Malik said.

"And believe me, he gets rather cranky if he doesn't get his coffee. So, I'll do you a favor this time."

"All the same…" Elle trailed off but he could tell she was wavering.

"Come on, what have I ever done to you to make you be so wary of me?" Her expression morphed to one of incredulity and just like that Malik felt his lips part in another smile.

"Duly noted. But, I'm serious here, Miss Roberts. Let me take the coffee. Go on and head back to the office. I'll even let you snag a twenty minute nap, how's that?"

"As if you could." Elle scoffed.

"Alliana watches me like a hawk, and Priya is worse."

"I promise that I will make sure neither of them bother you." Malik insisted, raising his hand in a mock gesture of honesty.

Elle frowned at him, and the look over her face was so endearing that Malik was tempted to close the space between them, just a little. Finally, she sighed before pushing the cup into his awaiting hands.

"Alright, but if Priya breaks my neck, you're paying for the funeral services." Elle said glumly.

"Don't be so morbid, Miss Roberts." Malik chuckled, taking in the hot cup of coffee and heading towards the door.

He pushed it open and allowed Elle past, "Go on ahead. I'll see you later."

Elle nodded, giving him a last look of uncertainty before smiling slightly. The simple change over her face did something to Malik he hadn't quite expected and when she thanked him, he couldn't help but watch as she walked off.

It was strange, but he found himself missing out on her expressions already.

Oh well.

And with that, Malik headed off in another direction to ponder how to make his big reveal, burning his tongue when he took a swift sip of his coffee.

Chapter 7

Twenty minutes, as it happened, was exactly what Elle needed. Being a secretary to a powerful man meant that she needed to be aware of his every move almost every second of every day, which was hilarious considering that fact that she hadn't even met him.

To her relief, Alliana and Priya had offered strict assistance in allowing her to do her job—even purchasing a new phone for her specifically to be used when she was working on matters involving the Sheikh.

It was somewhat overwhelming. Since she had started working here, she had gotten a full-makeover, gotten an entire new wardrobe and even a new phone. She felt both pampered and burdened with insane pressure.

It made no sense why they would put so much effort into her. That was the case, until Alliana barged in, just five minutes after Elle had woken up from her nap, to announce that the Sheikh was arriving.

"Straighten your desk, woman!" Alliana hissed, arriving to spruce up the otherwise immaculate office.

Elle organized her desk, watching the blonde woman scramble around back and forth, spraying a fine smelling mist around the office from a glass bottle and wrenching apart the curtains near the windows.

"The Sheikh is just minutes outside the door and you're gawking like a simpleton!"

At the announcement, Elle felt urgency spur her just as swiftly, and when Alliana looked over her, she gave her a nod of approval, which was more than Elle had ever gotten since her make-over.

"Alright, he'll be here soon, head over to the kitchen and bring a tall glass of Evian water and a slice of cucumber. The drink *cannot* be warmer than ice cold, do you understand? But so help me if I find an ice cube in that glass, I will personally *murder you.* Got it?"

Elle paled, nodding swiftly before escaping out the door, heading straight toward the stairs and making her way towards the kitchen.

At first, she nearly cried when she realized that the Evian water was bottled up near the back storage area, but she felt relief calm her when she noticed a stash of bottles in the very back of the immense five-star refrigerator.

Pushing aside vegetable trays and employee drinks, Elle snagged a bottle and grabbed a fresh cucumber.

As she sliced the vegetable, Elle couldn't help but keep an eye out for Malik. It was usually when she was scrambling for stuff that he would show up to laugh at her or distract her with his idiotic—and incredibly attractive—voice.

In fact, she wouldn't be surprised if he walked in right then and there to watch her grab a slice of cucumber and stick it in the tall crystal glass.

Instead, Malik was missing and Elle felt strangely confused at his absence. She did admit that she wanted to thank him for allowing her a little rest, even though he could be an arrogant prick, he didn't have to help her like that. Maybe he wasn't so bad after all.

Brushing thoughts of Malik away from her mind, Elle began to head back to the office, keeping her eyes fixed ahead even while she heard other employees whisper amongst themselves.

When she finally arrived, she was mortified to notice that she was practically shaking and that her palms were moist. Wiping them on her jacket, Elle proceeded to enter the suite and then toward the office.

As expected, Alliana was still there but she could be heard from behind the opened glass doors. The curtains were pulled aside somewhat and Elle spotted Alliana's slim and sharp figure through the sheer fabric.

"Absolutely, I'll be sure to pass the message along." The woman was saying.

"Anything else, Your Excellency?"

"That'll be all." She heard another voice say and for a moment, Elle paused. That voice sounded familiar…?

Shaking her head, Elle disregarded the strange sense of recognition before approaching the door.

She heard Alliana offer a final phrase in Arabic and suddenly she was walking out the door. When Alliana pushed past the curtains, she glanced at Elle with a look of exasperation.

"Don't just stand there, you twit. That should've been in there ten minutes ago!" She exclaimed quietly, pointing at the glass in Elle's hands before urging her through the door.

"Remember the rules!" Alliana said before Elle was suddenly past the curtains.

The office was bright now that the windows were without their curtains and when Elle approached she noticed that there were three men. All of them were dressed in fine robes and suits, appearing regal and powerful.

Elle had no idea which was which, until she noticed the one in the center who was busy staring out the window behind him,

Do not speak to the Sheikh unless spoken to.

Do not look at the Sheikh directly.

Do not touch the Sheikh in any manner whatsoever.

The two other men, Elle guessed they were guards, watched her intently. With a meek bow, the young woman placed the tall glass of water over a coaster on the immense wooden desk. She was already spinning around to run off until she heard one of them speak.

"Just a moment," and Elle froze in her spot, not daring to turn around. The sensation of being caught in the spotlight made her blood thrum in her ears.

The owner of the voice said a few other things in Arabic and Elle felt her skin become hyper aware when she heard a rustle of movement. The two men filed out of the room, not sparing her a glance before they closed the curtains and the glass doors.

"Are you going to stand there all day or are you going to come here?" A huge wave of déjà vu washed over Elle, making her heart stop and disbelief bleed into her mind.

Slowly, her body spun despite her shock and when she finally turned around it was to see the last person she had expected to see.

"M…Malik?" Elle stammered out, not believing the sight before her for a moment.

The Sheikh's face broke into an amused grin and the expression was so... *Malik* the doubt nearly left her completely.

"Miss Roberts, a pleasure to meet you finally."

Chapter 8

I'm going to kill him.

It was a thought that constantly jumped into her mind for the next few days.

For the longest time, Elle didn't know *what* to feel. She was torn between humiliation and complete mind-boggling outrage. That idiot man made a *fool* out of her!

He had sat by this entire time, laughing and poking fun at her, listening to her complain about the Sheikh when *he was really the Sheikh all along!*

What kind of sick person thinks that's funny?

And then another thought hit her—he had talked about her boobs, and then she had *shoved the man out of the office.* She broke one of the most important rules already!

With a wail, Elle buried her face in her palms, wanting to remain in the bathroom stall and just die in there because she had been *played.*

Yes, Elle wanted to kill him, but it's not like she could now!

Considering he was one of the most powerful clients associated with her uncle. And all this time, she had been meandering about and talking to him as though he was just any other man.

Ugh. She had even *fantasized* about him!

All of this was so wrong, so horribly wrong, and yet Elle knew she would have to return to her office and face Malik—no, the *Sheikh*—and hopefully try not to tackle him to the ground.

Then again, it was not like she would anyway. Sure she liked to talk big but she could never do anything, not even back in high school.

Alex had once laughed when she had cowered in her room one day after a fight with her best friend, Molly.

"Come on, little owl. Time to set things right." He had said.

The abrupt memory stopped her dead in her tracks and for a long moment, Elle just sat there waiting for the clench in her chest to disappear. It had been nearly a year since Alex broke up with her and left to go study in some university far away.

A year ago, she had been contemplating places where they would spend time together; she had even gone so far as to imagine how their wedding would be like.

A year ago, Elle had been perfectly happy living in a small little town with her boyfriend of three years and with her wild mane of brown curls to bounce over her head.

Now, she was in a large city, single, and her hair now fell down her cheeks in loose waves. She had changed… or she thought she did.

She had left that town and the comfort of her parent's home to pursue a life of independence. A life without Alex, a life where she could be happy on her own. She looked different; everything around her was different…

All except for the single little fact that she was still hiding from the world.

Come on, little owl. Time to set things right.

Clenching her fists and taking a breath, Elle pushed herself off the women's toilet.

When she came face to face with the long mirror, she fixed herself a look of determination.

"*I may not look like the women out there, but I've got something none of them have.*"

Malik rose a brow, "Oh, and what's that?"

Elle fixed him a defiant stare, "Determination. So you can go tell the Sheikh that I'm not going to get beaten that easily."

Squaring her shoulders, Elle walked out of the bathroom more than ready to face this challenge on her own, even if she was a little bit scared.

Chapter 9

For the following week, Elle followed orders and managed all the documents given to her with new found zeal. The Sheikh had become exactly what she wanted him to be: her employer.

No longer did he point and laugh at her whenever she made a mistake, instead he'd fix her a simple gaze that spoke of patience beyond his years. The man who would banter and spark silly arguments with her was no longer around and while a bit surprising that that same man now gave her eloquent orders and spoke to her clearly, it was sobering.

Still, there were moments where he infuriated her. Moments where he would pull stunts like decide to abruptly cancel a meeting even though there were only ten minutes to give a warning to all participants and Elle would make mad-dash calls to inform people of great status that the Sheikh could not attend and that he offered his apologies (yeah right).

Or sometimes he would appear, dressed completely like how she saw him the first time and she would almost greet him like she did, or she would almost respond to a comment he made with a snarky look.

She caught herself from snapping back when the Sheikh had told her to fix him a new cup of coffee. *Do it yourself, Malik.* She almost hissed before she paused, and was suddenly being stared at by the man in question.

"Problem, Miss Roberts?" He asked and it was so strange how he could be two different people at the exact same time.

"It's nothing…" She said before taking a step back.

"Miss Roberts?"

He called and Elle could feel something start in her chest. He did not say her name like he usually did—stiff and mechanical as the Sheikh would, or mocking and probing like Malik would. No. He spoke her name gently and the tone of his voice made her feel something she hadn't quite expected.

"Yes?" She finally spoke when she realized he was waiting for her to acknowledge him.

"I will be taking a trip to Bellevue this weekend for an important meeting with some clients. Specifically to handle the Baudelaire case."

Elle recognized the name from one of the files and remembered that their firm would be doing taking the defense.

"I was wondering if you would come along with me."

The request took her by surprise. Elle had never traveled, only doing so once before she moved to Seattle with her uncle.

"You want me to go with you?"

Malik nodded, "Yes. This is the sort of thing I would require of my secretary."

And suddenly the whole tone of the conversation returned to that strained professionalism between them. What it was before… Elle wasn't sure she wanted to give it a name.

"For how long?"

"A week at most."

Did she want to spend time alone with this man? Elle wasn't sure, but she hardly believed she had an option to say no.

"Alright."

And then he nodded and waved her away.

Elle gave a short bow before she turned and walked off, hoping that the trembling in her hands wasn't visible to his scrutiny.

Chapter 10

"We're lost."

"We're not lost."

For the twelve millionth time, Elle couldn't help but curse the man sitting at her side inwardly. This man was gifted with a ridiculous amount of money. He had protection, he had prospects. But the bloody idiot had no sense of direction at all.

Of all the idiotic reasons to not take a plane out—Elle had even gotten excited to fly on a private jet—none would be enough to satisfy why Malik was allowed to take one of the company's expensive cars and decide to drive the couple to the city.

Elle had hoped to a ride in luxury, considering all the stuff Malik had put her through since she had become his secretary, and instead she got hours of awkward silence and finally facing the fact that they had been driving for far too long.

"Bellevue was only a four hour drive, your excellency," Elle said, trying to keep her voice at a respectful decibel.

"And yet we've been driving for nine. Please just face it, we're lost."

"Miss Roberts, for the last time, we're not lost." Malik stated firmly, yet whatever humor there was in his voice was completely depleted.

He was also steaming in frustration and the close proximity and growing tension was giving them both a high dosage of cabin fever.

"Look, with all due respect, could we just turn around and head back to that shack—"

"We are *not* asking for directions, Miss Roberts. So you can take that idea and shove it."

Irritation blossomed through Elle's nerves, making her see red for a split moment. Unable to handle his bitten words, Elle faced him with a simmering glare.

"Oh, wonderful. I never thought the stereotype reached your lands, but wow, you sure showed me."

"What stereotype?"

Malik shot back, glaring into the open road ahead of them. This road didn't look anything like the highway and honestly, those thunderheads above only promised dark omens.

"That egotistical men can't handle asking for directions because they take it as a blow to their pathetic pride!" Elle finally snapped.

"Watch it, habibi." Malik huffed.

"Or what, you'll *fire* me?" Elle continued with a strange sense of daring.

"Well, by all means do so because after I stop working for you, I'll find my own way back home while you continue driving in circles!"

"I'm tempted to just drop you off here so you can go and do that!"

He rolled his eyes and Elle let out a grunt of aggravation.

"Then what is stopping you?" She exclaimed.

"You can just as easily find another girl to do my job. And she'll be much prettier and quieter and will just bow her head and fill all your needs!"

"You had me at the 'quieter' part," Malik said coldly.

"Maybe I will do just that."

He could have slapped her and it would've hurt less. Elle fell silent at that, feeling absurdly stung by his words.

Thunder rumbled in the distance and little specks of rain began to stick to the windshield. All around them were large trees that loomed like huge green giants above them and for a moment, Elle wished he would just drop her off so she could hide the tears threatening to burn down her eyes.

She felt ridiculous.

Why would that make her hurt?

There was no need to feel so wounded by such a selfish man.

"What's this, the thought of losing your job actually registering in your head?" Malik continued.

Elle said nothing, sternly keeping her body tight against the passenger door, her gaze outside the window.

To her dismay, her emotions were not as invisible as she wished they would be and when she dared breathe, the sound came out with a slight sniffle that alerted the man.

"Miss Roberts?"

"Just leave me alone for once, would you? You've said enough."

"I don't understand—are you *crying*?"

Elle clenched her eyes shut, feeling the tears cascade down her cheeks before she brushed them away harshly.

"This whole thing was just a bad idea," she muttered.

"What traveling with me?" Malik voiced.

"Taking this stupid job!" She finally admitted.

When she faced him, he was giving her a stunned expression.

"What kind of sick person tricks their employee like the way you tricked me? I don't care where you come from, because where I come from that is a seriously wrong thing to do. You laughed at me, you mocked me, all the while you were the Sheikh, and I was making a *fool* of myself at *your* entertainment!"

Malik looked away to look at the road and to her mortification, she realized he was pulling over to the side of the road.

When he put the car in park, Elle found her chance to put some much needed distance between them. Without warning, she unhooked her seatbelt and unlocked her door.

The door gave with a push and Elle was stumbling out. A chilly breeze wrapped around her and she could feel icy drops of rain fall over her body.

"Hey!" She heard, before she heard Malik's door open too.

"Where are you going?"

"Away from you, obviously!" She called back, angry at the tears coursing down her cheeks, angry at the fact that even now she was running away to hide.

She heard his footsteps catch up before she felt him grab her wrist. *Do not touch the Sheikh in any manner whatsoever.* Yanking her wrist away, Elle whirled around to glare at him. That slightest touch of skin on skin had burned her. It had made her feel something she knew she couldn't toward this man.

"Do not touch me!"

She cried, trying not to care about the vulnerable flicker in his dark eyes, the way his full lips parted and how his shoulders slumped at her rejection.

"I'm not allowed to touch you, get it? Ever!"

"Miss Roberts," Malik began.

"Don't—please just don't," Elle said, shaking her head.

The moisture in the air was making her hair frizz, and a gust of wind cast her brown locks around her face.

Hugging herself, Elle wanted nothing more than to become small and to be blown away with the wind.

"I didn't ask for this, Malik. I don't want to feel this."

"Feel what?"

He asked and his voice was also small, and she was reminded that he was just a man. That far away from titles and gold and impressionable status, he was just a man.

"This!" She said waving her hands between her and him.

"You have infuriated me for these past couple of months. You tricked me, you *lied* to me! But you also made me laugh even when I wanted to punch you—okay? No one's ever made me feel that way. And then I go and find out that you're my boss, that you're The Sheikh! That you're fucking *untouchable* and that I'm just a white girl who can't ever have anything to do with your world… And when I can finally say that I feel objective, you go and you hurt me again!"

He took a step toward her, and the look over his eyes was absolutely wretched.

"If it's about what I said in the car—"

Elle didn't give him the chance.

"It's about literally everything you've ever done! I don't know if I can trust you. I don't know if I can trust myself around you! I can't do this. I can't because the last time I let myself—" she stopped herself short, feeling surprised even at the words falling from her mouth.

What am I saying?

"Let yourself what, Elle?" Malik asked, and she felt her name on his tongue as intimately as if he had touched her.

She didn't like the look in his eye, the look that was somewhat hopeful, even wishing.

"Do you… have a crush on me?"

The way he said it made it seem too juvenile. It made her feel like she was back in high school. A huge wave of revulsion and embarrassment washed over her and Elle could feel herself recoil from him.

Did he think this was a joke? This was another game to him?

This can't be happening.

"Just, leave me alone."

She said and when she turned around, she could feel the rain fall with more definition around them. Elle wanted nothing more than to disappear. She wanted to fly away.

Instead, she felt his hand wrap around hers again, pulling her back with surprising force.

When Elle whirled around, she was more than prepared to shout at him, to hurt him with her hands for the wounds he had caused her with his words.

Instead, he was suddenly gripping around her jaw, and pulling her up towards his face.

His lips were hot against hers, hot and bruising. Hot and needy. Hot and amazing.

Elle's mind was spinning, her knees felt shaky and wobbly, all she could do was cling to his shirt to keep from falling over.

Malik pressed kiss after kiss against her mouth, made her feel so strange and light, so confused and excited. What was going on…?

Finally he broke away and she could feel the icy rain dig into her skin and jolt her to reality.

Before she could push away, he was burning his dark eyes against her green ones.

"I like you too, Elle." He said and the confession stunned her into another silence that he was more than happy to fill with another mind-boggling kiss.

I like you too, Elle.

I like you too, Elle.

And suddenly Elle realized that what she had been feeling wasn't just a simple attraction, and now that Malik was kissing her, Elle realized with some disbelief that his words made her feel… happy.

Chapter 11

It took off far too fast, but it was like she was being whisked into a storm of fire and delicious heat. Before she could fully understand what was happening, Malik was leading her by the lips toward the car.

She stumbled after him, wanting to keep her mouth on his and allowing this strange sensation to carry her far away from the pain of the past few months.

They moved back inside the car, and when Malik opened the backseat doors, Elle was reluctant to part from him for a moment.

Finally there and safe from the incoming storm, Elle only had a moment to breathe slowly before Malik was sliding against her and pressing another amazing kiss to her lips.

Elle moaned against his mouth, more out of surprise and now that her head wasn't as preoccupied with his words and more with what was happening between them.

"M-Malik," she began against his lips.

He paused for a moment, breathing hard against her while his hands were flush against her ribs. She was so close to pushing him away, so close to ending their little charade before it got too far when she saw it.

Saw the familiar rawness in his eyes that told her that he wasn't so far off from where she was in terms of feelings. That same pain that she had seen for months in her own eyes since Alex left her was now being reflected back at her through his eyes.

He was also hurt… and it was driving him just as crazy as this strange attraction between the two of them. And that was when Elle knew she couldn't stop herself from connecting with this man.

When her mouth met his, the kiss was different. Different because now there was a different desperation behind her tongue and when his lips parted to meet hers, she caught that same desperation against his.

It was bitter, it was heady, and it made Elle want to make it all go away.

The kiss intensified, and their breathing grew haggard as each touch they caused over their skin made desire flow like lava. She couldn't remember who touched bare flesh first, but the next thing she knew, her clothes were being peeled off her sweat-sticky skin.

Her shirt went first, and when she felt Malik's lips burn down her throat toward her breasts, Elle let out a gasp that ripped into his hands and made him grasp her closer to him.

His shirt came next, and soon her hands were running over the sharp planes of his muscular back. When Malik's teeth found the edge of her bra, Elle was collapsing back against the lush leather seat, back arching to expose her to his attention.

His fingers made quick work of the fabric containing her and when the strap of her bra came undone, she felt her breast spill out of the underwear and into Malik's hands.

His thumbs and forefingers found her nipples easily, teasing the puckered flesh and sending jolt after jolt of pleasure through Elle's system. When his mouth closed around one of the dusky rose buds, Elle let out a cry that was muffled by a crackle of thunder.

His tongue flashed over her skin, gently laving over the peaks of her breasts and eliciting electric sparks beneath her flesh. Her nerve endings were on overload, filling her to the brim with the intoxicating desire to pull him closer.

Their movements became less focused, clumsier now that they were both on a one way road to a singular climax. Her hands yanked into his dark hair, the moisture of the rain making her snag on his tangled hair almost too hard. He let out a sharp hiss at that, but said nothing.

Malik's hands had found the hem of her pants quick, and when he pulled them down, his nails had accidentally raked against the sensitive flesh of her rear and thighs.

Elle let out a groan at that but felt the pain ebb away into a sting that could only be satisfied the more he touched her.

She lifted her knee to help him pull her pants off, and ended up accidentally kicking him in the ribs.

"Sorry!" She began, but he gave her a smirk instead and for the first moment since they began, she thought she saw the old Malik in how he loomed over her.

A giggle erupted from her lips when his fingers pressed against a tickle spot by her hips, her body jerking at the contact.

"You're ticklish?" He asked.

"Don't you dare," Elle hissed, already throwing her hands to catch his before he dared do anything that would break the mood. Malik laughed throatily, swooping down to press another hot kiss against her mouth.

Elle moaned when his hands proceeded to run up and down her sides, paying close attention to her breasts before he made his way further down.

His fingers trailed teasingly close where she needed it most, and Elle's hips bucks the closer he inched near her folds, grazing but never touching them.

He was teasing her, for sure, and it sparked a competitive fire in Elle's blood that made her drag her own palms down his skin before meeting the clothed erection straining through his expensive suit trousers.

Malik let out a yelp when she grasped him and when he looked back up at her, she was smirking back at him.

"Oh, so that's how you want to do it."

He said with a wicked smile, and with a decisive tug, Malik pulled his fingers around her drenched sex and pressed two fingers knuckle-deep inside of Elle.

Elle let out a gasp at the intrusion, feeling her body shudder with each thrust he pushed against her. She had almost forgotten about his erection in her hand until she gave him an involuntary squeeze.

He moaned above her and the sound snapped her back to attention. Her hands found the buttons of his trousers, quickly unbuckling the belt and pulling down the zipper before she hooked her thumbs at his hips.

"Elle, are you—" Malik began, his words stopping short when she pulled the fabric of his pants and underwear down with one yank.

His fingers paused their thrusting and when their gazes met, Elle could only smile at him before her fingers grasped around his length.

He was thick, long, and hot and the skin felt silky smooth at her touch. Gentle but hurriedly, Elle wasted no time to pump him, remembering how she had gained her experience with Alex and how he had loved it when she went fast.

Instead, Malik reached a hand down and closed his fingers around her wrist, eyes clenched shut tight.

"E-easy," He wheezed. "Not so fast."

"Am I hurting you?"

She asked, feeling reproachful now that they took a moment to reflect.

Malik gave her a one-sided smile.

"I'm fine," he said, "just… go a little slower."

When he released her, Elle resumed her caress over his skin, sliding her palm and fingers up and down his length with more deliberate strokes.

"Like that," he said, eyes still shut but loosening into a pleasured expression.

His face was so vulnerable, Elle could only stare in awe.

"Like this." He said and suddenly, his fingers were pumping into her.

The sensations made her grip on him stutter to a stop before she picked up to her rhythmic pace. Carefully, she tightened her hold around him, and in response, Malik pumped his fingers into her a little harder.

Elle could feel Malik thrust his hips against her hand just as she wiggled and grinded her hips against his, their gasps and moans growing together the more they moved.

Just as Elle could feel the beginning of her orgasm approach, Malik suddenly stopped, and Elle let out a swift groan of protest.

"Not like this," Malik sighed out.

"I want to be inside you when you come."

His words only made her body feel further high-strung, made her muscles coil in anticipation for the pleasure that was to come.

Even as she felt that way, she felt a rush of heat burn against her cheeks, made her feel so strangely shy beneath his heated gaze.

"How could you say things like that…?" She muttered.

"That's embarrassing."

Malik didn't seem to be expecting this and when he glanced down at her, she felt like she was being revered all over again.

Finally, a small smile passed over his lips and it was the first time she ever saw him smile at her like that.

"You're something else, Miss Roberts."

"S-shut up, Malik."

She muttered, but her embarrassment melted away when she felt his thumb land over her clit and rub leisure circles against it.

"My name," he murmured, "is Zayn. I'd like for you to call me that."

"Ah-ha—ah—aahh…" Elle moaned, lips parted to let out her moans of wanton pleasure.

Malik pressed a little harder against her and Elle's hips gave a rather sharp buck at that, her fingers falling from around his member to grasp to his shoulder.

"Say it, Elle."

It only occurred to her then that he meant for her to say his name.

"Z-Zayn," she breathed out, her breath hiccupping in her chest as he gave her another rub.

She could feel it… the start of her orgasm just creeping up.

"Say it again…"

"Zayn," she moaned, bucking against him again to make the friction harder.

She wanted to take that plunge right now. Of course, Malik would pull away, and when she blinked through half-lidded eyes, he was smiling down at her widely.

Before she could yell at him to keep moving, she suddenly felt him shift his hips, aligning himself against her assuredly.

Elle's eyes widened when she realized he was just against her entrance.

"Ready?" He breathed.

"Zayn!" His name exploded from her lips just as he sheathed himself deep within her.

The sensation of being filled by him made Elle arch her back and let out a cry she had never heard from herself ever before.

Alex had been thick, but he wasn't particularly long. Whereas Malik, on the other hand, had pushed himself so deeply inside her, Elle could feel him in her throat.

His girth, while dense, was not unpleasant, yet it took a few moments of heavy breathing and clenching hard to each other for Elle to become accustomed to his fullness.

Carefully, Malik pumped against her, keeping his strokes short against her so that she could get used to how deep he penetrated her.

Each graze of his tip brushed against her womb, making Elle feel like all the blood in her body would pulse against her head before rushing back down and then back to her head all over again.

"Elle," Malik breathed against her throat, his hands bruising tight against her hips and against her arched back.

"Relax."

Elle took in his words and had to physically pry one of her hands from his scalp, where she had been gripping to for her life.

He pumped against her once more, pressing soothing kisses to her throat before meeting her parted lips deliciously.

His mouth worked over hers, bringing her back to him and allowing her to reciprocate his kisses with growing passion.

Before long, he was fluidly pulling back before sliding into her again, memorizing with his hands how her body would convulse and arc with every thrust like a wave.

"Oh," Elle moaned after he pulled away, dragging one of his fingers to tease her clit.

"Oh, Zayn…"

His movements, while slow, were steadily driving her mad and if he didn't increase his pace soon, Elle would probably explode with frustration.

"P-please," she begged. He slowed down and Elle nearly shouted.

"What is it?" He asked her softly.

Elle reached back up around his jaw, cradling his face with her hands as she brought him up to her mouth, "Faster, *faster*."

Malik groaned into her tongue, dragging one of his hands down from her hip to grip to her thigh. He pulled the limb further up, adjusting their position so he could meet her demands.

He gave one particularly strong thrust and Elle was letting out an amazing scream, her eyes popping open to behold trickles of rain and gales of wind ripping around their small car right now.

She wasn't sure if the car was shaking hard because of the wind or because of how powerfully Malik was pounding into her.

Her entire body was on fire, her limbs quivering with every hot flash of pleasure, and suddenly Malik's thumb was flicking harder against her sex, driving her into her orgasm with the force of an explosion.

Until, finally, Elle felt her walls clamp down against Malik's length, and she was riding out the most powerful climax she had ever felt in her life.

She distinctly heard someone calling Malik's name over and over, and it wasn't until she felt her mind settle down from the white-hot pleasure that she realized it was her own voice pleading with Malik to keep going.

Suddenly, Malik pushed harder and harder against her, and Elle felt her body spasm with each thrust until he was shuddering powerful, his body wracking as he let out a low groan that grew into a shout.

Without warning, he pulled away from her and Elle felt the absence of him from her body immediately. She almost asked what was wrong until she felt something hot slap and spread over her belly and chest.

Elle lay there gasping, fighting to catch her breath even as she tried to glance down and find out what had happened.

Eventually, she straightened up against him, felt Malik droop his forehead against her shoulder and his sweat soaked hair clung to her skin.

When she glanced down, she saw long lines of white come over her belly.

"You…pulled it out?" She asked.

"Didn't… bring a condom." He replied, just as out of breath as she was.

"Idiot," she scolded, but was smiling when he glanced at her.

"I'm on the pill."

Malik returned her smile with one of his own, "One can never be too careful."

"Well, now," she paused to swallow back some air. "I'm all sticky."

"Don't complain," Malik retorted.

Elle rolled her eyes before lifting her hands up toward his face. He met her kiss half-way, their lips making echoes of the slaps that had occurred between their bodies just moments prior.

"That was… amazing." He muttered against her lips.

"Hmm…" Elle hummed, relishing the warmth between them despite the slight discomfort of the lack of air.

It was almost stifling, but she was pulsing and throbbing with so much ecstasy, it was hard to care.

Eventually, caring had to come after their bodies recovered.

When Malik pulled away, Elle was forced to think of what they had just done, and what it meant for them in the future.

"Malik..." She spoke and she was pushing herself up to sit against the seat. She winced when she felt the damp between her legs shift weirdly as she moved.

Malik was already pulling out a packet of towlettes from the passenger door, offering it to her without a word. He seemed to be realizing what they had done as well.

Elle kept silent until she had cleaned herself up from the remains of Malik's come, tossing the soiled tissues into a compartment he had pointed out to her quietly.

It was getting dark and the wind continued to thrash hard against the car. She wasn't worried though, this was the sort of vehicle that could handle a little storm. What did worry her was Malik's abrupt silence.

"Can we talk for a second?" She asked after a moment.

"Depends on what you want to say," he replied.

Elle frowned, the endorphins rushing through her system made her feel light and flighty, but she knew that if they didn't deal with this now... it would only get worse.

Huh... not running and hiding now are we, little owl?

"Did you mean what you said?" She asked cautiously, as if she wasn't sure she wanted to do this.

"...Out there?"

Then he turned and looked at her, *really* looked at her and despite having watched each other come apart in throes of passion, Elle felt more exposed under his stare than she had before.

"That I liked you?"

The words made her feel that same embarrassment from before, and she nearly looked away shyly. Elle stamped down the urge instead, meeting his gaze head on.

She nodded, but couldn't help but fidget and grip to the edge of her leather seat.

Malik moved then, breaching the space between them to cradle her cheeks in his hands. He hardly touched her, but there was intent in his hold and passion hidden within the darkness of his eyes.

"Of all the times I had lied to you…" he trailed off, jaw clenching for a moment.

"And I am sorry for that… for lying to you, tricking you. I have this idiotic tendency to act before I think. But if I can be honest with you, Elle, it's that when I told you I liked you I wasn't lying. I honestly liked you the moment you waltzed in and talked back to me, even though you had no idea who I was, you stood your ground. So, yes, Elle. I meant it."

A small smile leaked passed her lips and she saw him smile back, that same charming smile he had given her when they had been connected and writhing together.

It had just happened between them, but Elle felt her body react at his touch. A shiver began deep within her to spread everywhere else and she took a shuddering breath when his smile wavered slightly to reveal a similar expression.

"Where do we go from here?" Elle muttered quietly.

Malik paused, just inches from kissing her before he pulled away.

The anticipation in her body slowed to a cold stop when Malik sighed slowly and peeled his skin away from her.

"You want my honesty, right, Elle?"

Elle nodded despite feeling a strange sense of foreboding deep in her stomach.

He looked away, dark eyes shadowed by the curls of his hair, "I have too many secrets… too many things that you should stay away from. And while I want nothing more than to take a step in your direction… I don't know."

When he looked at her, Elle felt as though someone had placed a thick wall between the two of them.

"I just don't know."

Chapter 12

By the time morning came, they came to discover that the car had very little gas at all. If they were lucky it would be enough to take them a few miles closer to the next town. The problem was that they didn't know how much farther the next town could be.

The tension between the two hadn't really improved, and since they had collided, it had now become more awkward than before. There was too much unsaid, too much that they didn't know. They had taken a hasty step into unknown territory and were now paying the price.

Elle couldn't help but kick herself mentally the entire time she sat back in the car and waited for Malik to say something. Her nerve and courage that came the night before was all snuffed out, leaving her to sit back in her damp clothes and hope this all ended quickly.

She felt insanely torn in so many places. The main reason was because she couldn't ignore the fact that she had slept with her boss. The next thing that would plague her was the fact that her body wasn't too keen on forgetting *exactly* how she had slept with her boss, and memories of their bodies rubbing together in hard thrusts left her aching and sore with the remnants of desire.

Another part would then squabble with the other factors, insisting that what could happen to her now that she had broached this forbidden boundary she was doomed to face the consequences.

What consequences? Elle didn't really know.

All she knew was that she had probably broken nearly all the Rules in one fell swoop.

Except that one.

With a groan, Elle recounted that one particular rule, the one that she must attend to the Sheikh's every needs. Well technically she did sort of do that, even if it meant she also attended to her needs as well. She just hoped that one little rule would be enough to keep her safe from being hunted down by Arab families.

That was another thing. What if their actions caused some kind of terrible situation between the two countries?

When Elle had done her own research, she had basically discovered that Sheikh Zayn Abd al Malik was practically a prince from his country.

Did she just have mind shattering, world spinning sex with a Prince?

He probably had diplomatic immunity, but she sure as hell didn't!

What would this mean for her?

A knock on the glass of her window nearly spooked Elle from her seat and just then she realized that she had been busy gnawing at her thumbnail anxiously.

Glancing up, she saw Malik, standing outside and offering her a water bottle that he must have gotten from the trunk.

Swallowing thickly, she recognized the little truce offering and opened her door. Malik stepped back for her to stand up, and there was a silence between them that was almost as deafening as the sound of insects and forest life in the woods around them.

"Here." Malik sighed.

Elle took the water bottle wordlessly. They shifted awkwardly for a moment until Elle couldn't take it any longer.

"Look, I need to know…" She began and when he looked at her, she nearly faltered.

"I want to make sure that what we did… that wasn't a mistake… was it?"

He crossed his arms, shifting his weight against his heels.

"Do you regret it?"

Elle opened her mouth to speak, but the air caught in her throat. There was too much. Far too much she didn't know.

When she glanced away, Malik let out a slow sigh.

"Would you hate me if I told you I didn't?"

Elle snapped back toward him, green eyes wide.

"Why? Aren't you worried…? I mean, what do we do? Should I be worried about my job? Should I be worried if someone finds out? You probably have safety but I don't. In the end, I'm still a nobody from Issaquah, and you're a *Sheikh* from Dubai."

Malik took a step forward, his jaw tight with mild self-restraint, "See, that's what I don't care about. Do you know how many people in my life constantly remind me and use me for my title? My status? Everyone, Elle. Everyone I've ever met has only been interested in me because I have what I have… But you…? You and Avani…" he broke off, thick brows furrowing together.

Avani…?

And then Elle remembered. She knew Malik had been hurting, she knew the pain he was feeling, because she recognized it intimately.

She remembered how Avani had a baby the day Elle had arrived for her first day, remembered Malik's biting comment on the event instead of appearing happy for the woman. And it all clicked into place.

"You love her, don't you?"

Malik turned a rueful smile up at her, and he let out a soft laugh.

"She's not unlike you, you know. She was headstrong, always kept me in check. But she fell in love with some other bloke, and I was too late to tell her how I felt. That day when you walked in, I had been counting down the hours, hoping that she wouldn't show up—that she would stay far away because all she could ever talk about was how happy she was for having this baby, and I could only hate myself for hating it."

Suddenly he let out a short laugh.

"Then you walk in, wearing this awful two piece get-up and all I can think to myself is, my god there is no rest for me at all is there? You just waltzed in… and I liked you instantly."

Elle shook her head slowly, not making a certain connection, "Hold on… then why didn't you…?"

He filled in the words for her.

"Tell you that I was your boss? That I was the bloody Sheikh of Dubai? Because when you saw me you had *no clue* who I was and I couldn't remember the last time someone talked to me like a normal person. So yes, I lied to you, I tricked you…"

He stopped for a moment, and she could feel a twinge of something begin in her heart that she hadn't felt since before Alex left her.

"But that was because I didn't want you to lie and trick me."

Elle stared at him, stunned speechless as her mind traced his words and focused on the earnest gleam of his eyes.

In the pale sunlight of this dreary day, he still looked radiant, despite the wrinkled clothes and the bit of stubble growing over his jaw. How could someone so powerful look so vulnerable?

Slowly, Elle took a step closer, before nodding softly at him. Gingerly, she reached a hand out to catch his between her fingers.

It was odd, because she wasn't sure if she was doing the right thing, but she could feel his pulse against her fingertips and it was racing just as hard as hers was. Linking their fingers, Elle blinked back up at Malik before giving him a shaky smile.

"No more lies and tricks?"

She asked meekly and Malik returned her smile just as he took another step closer. Pressing his forehead against hers, Malik sighed and Elle could feel a bit of relief ease the tension burrowing in her shoulders.

"No more lies and tricks."

Chapter 13

It had taken the rest of the day to wait for someone to come help them. After finally reaching Alliana, the woman had asked them to turn on the GPS function in the car and use what little gas they had left to emit a signal—which was ridiculous to Elle, but she just went with it.

Hours later and several conversations later between Elle and Malik that allowed them to share more about one another, a team of Malik's guard arrived.

To Elle's dismay, Malik resumed his guise as the Sheikh, keeping firmly away from her and even addressing her formally in front of the caravan. The performance nearly broke at Elle's heart but one single glance of sincere apology from Malik managed to convince her to stay strong.

They rode off and made their way back to their city, where for the large remainder of the drive was spent with Malik making many phone calls to apologize for his absence during their client's meeting. Elle almost felt sorry for him, but when he glanced at her and she gave him a little smirk, he could only smirk back before continuing his slew of apologies.

They managed to stop at a motel in order to wash up and dress in clean clothes before continuing their journey back.

The entire ride back, Elle couldn't help but worry about what else would come.

Would she be pursuing a secret relationship with the Sheikh? Would that even work out?

There was still so much she didn't know, but she was willing to see how far they could be able to go—so long as they were together, and Elle supposed that wasn't so bad.

Chapter 14

It was ten at night by the time they made it back to the main building, and Elle was incredibly glad to see Priya and Alliana again—even if they weren't all that enthused with seeing her. Still Alliana expressed some appreciation that they didn't die, so that was that.

Priya, on the other hand, had glared at her viciously the moment they had approached and the strange hostility from the woman did not go unnoticed by Malik either.

Malik had pulled away from Elle, approaching the petite woman with soothing phrases spoken in rapid Arabic. That entire time, Priya kept a hard stare over Elle, as if she were trying to kill her with a single gaze and Elle honestly felt her stomach waver at the hard attention.

To her relief, Priya broke away from the conversation with Malik, fixing him a look of shame before she disappeared into the illustrious building.

"Is everything alright?"

Elle murmured as they made their way inside.

"Its fine," Malik replied just as quietly.

"I'll explain later."

Yet there was something in his voice that made Elle feel more than concerned. She kept her thoughts to herself, because that was not the time nor the place.

Soon, Elle was being escorted down toward a car, just an hour after they had arrived. Malik followed her to the doors where he spoke in swift Arabic to the men of his guard.

He looked back at her one more time.

"These men will take you home, Miss Roberts. If you encounter any issues, please be sure to call us. We'll talk more tomorrow."

I'll talk to you tomorrow.

Elle nodded, allowing herself to trust Malik's promise before disappearing behind sleek metal doors and the growl of expensive engines.

Just minutes later, Elle was at her apartment, exhausted beyond belief but glad that her Uncle was already asleep. It was almost 11:30 at night by the time Elle managed to collapse into her bed, her eyes flitting shut moments later.

Chapter 15

A strange buzzing woke her not long after Elle drifted off. Grogginess turned her limbs to jelly and when she managed to pull herself up and reach for the source of the buzzing—it was the phone Priya had purchased for her—Elle was surprised to find Malik's name on the surface.

Rubbing sleep out of her eyes, Elle pressed the green 'answer' button on the touchscreen before lifting the phone to her ear.

"Hello?"

"Elle, it's me." She heard and felt her heart jump to her throat. Of course it would be him. Still it was strange for him to call, even stranger to call at this hour.

"Malik, is everything alright?"

"It's fine." He replied shortly, and it was then that Elle noticed that his voice was lacking his usual emotion. He sounded flat… strange.

"Come outside."

"Wait—what? Where are you?" She whispered, already shifting off her mattress.

"Just come outside." He said and then she heard a couple of beeps signifying the call had ended.

Frowning, Elle stood up and grabbed a nearby bathrobe, placing her phone inside the pocket just in case she needed to call her Uncle.

She wobbled her way toward the door, feeling her body already protest loudly to every movement—specifically between her legs. When she reached the door, she felt a strange chill begin from her spine to the rest of her body.

The feeling to hide nearly choked her for a moment and she could only stare at the door ahead of her in surprise. Shaking her head, Elle reached for the door and opened it.

Malik was standing just outside her door and Elle gasped in surprise. His body was dressed in a black cotton shirt and jeans, looking nothing like the mogul she had worked for several weeks now.

He stared at her with a simple appraisal, glancing at her body before meeting her gaze head on.

"Malik, what's going on?" Elle whispered, taking a step outside and closing the door behind her.

There was a chill in the air and it made her wrap her arms around her body.

"Come with me," he said instead, reaching a palm toward her.

"Hold on, can you at least answer the question?" She asked, feeling so strangely distrustful of him.

Her eyes trailed over his face, he didn't look any different… except his eyes stared at her without any of the warmth he had given her before.

"I'll answer your questions later, but you have to come with me. Now."

He took a step closer, no longer waiting for her to take his hand. When he grabbed her, his grip was tight and cold, Elle nearly wrenched herself away from him.

"What's the matter with you?" She asked, feeling panic begin to spread through her chilled skin.

Malik gave her a forceful tug, urging her down the stairs of the apartment without another word.

"Malik, what is it, you're starting to freak me out."

He remained silent even after they reached the ground floor. When they approached his car, Elle felt a continuous tug of worry when she noticed the vehicle looked like any other, nothing like his expensive station wagons or mercedes benz.

He opened the passenger door before nearly shoving her in and Elle let out a small yelp when he slammed the door shut. She had no idea what was going on… and frankly it was starting to scare her.

When he slid into the driver's seat, he wasted no time pulling the car out of park and slamming his foot into the gas. The car jolted forward, throwing Elle hard against her seat.

Frightened, Elle stayed quiet, sending panicked glances to the silent man now driving them away. Elle finally decided to try to speak to him again, maybe get some kind of response.

"...Zayn?"

"Do not call me that," Malik snapped bitingly.

"You will *never* call me that."

Alarmed and frightened, Elle became mute, sitting half-frozen in her seat. She had no idea what was going on or what was happening… something wasn't right.

Reaching into her pocket, Elle dragged her fingers toward the 'silent' trigger in her phone.

Once she was sure it would make no noise, Elle shifted her body against the chair away from Malik.

"What are you doing?" He asked abruptly and Elle stiffened.

"I'm…I'm tired." She lied shakily.

"I'm sure you'll explain when I wake up."

This seemed to satisfy him because he didn't ask any more questions. Elle carefully pulled her phone out, and lowered the backlight down to a faint dimness. She hoped he didn't notice and waited a long moment in case he did.

When there was nothing but the faint growl of the engine between them, Elle pressed in her passcode with her thumb, swiftly searching for her contacts before finding Alliana's number.

If he wouldn't give her answers, maybe the woman will.

The Sheikh is taking me somewhere. I don't know where. What's going on?

She didn't wait long for a response.

Where are you?

Elle glanced out the window, noticing how they were now turning into the highway.

I think he's taking me north... we just got on the highway.

Suddenly she got another message, this time it was from Priya.

What car are you in?

This confused Elle, but she glanced around, her eyes finding the make of the care in the little symbol on the dashboard.

It's a Ford. I think.

Minutes later, Elle received another message.

Don't do anything stupid.

What the hell did that mean?

Wracking her brain and feeling abandoned, Elle just sat back, hoping for answers sooner rather than later.

Chapter 16

"Wake up." She heard, and Elle was suddenly being pulled out from her seat.

Blinking away spots, the smell of pine and earth surrounded her, and when she put her feet outside she felt cold earth between her toes.

It was practically pitch dark if not for the lights of the car. Elle groaned softly, her body protesting the hard movements from Malik's manhandling.

"Wha…? Where are we? Malik?"

Elle murmured but wasn't answered before she was being lead away from the car and toward a dark structure up ahead. She didn't remember falling asleep. What's worse was how terribly cold it was.

Before long, Elle was shivering hard in Malik's grip. He led her toward the structure and after her feet stumbled over one of the wooden planks of the stairs did she realize they were in a cabin.

"What is this place, Malik?" Elle asked, feeling sleep disappear once her body realized this wasn't a regular place.

"Why are we here?"

"Silence." He ordered swiftly just as he opened the door and shoved her inside.

Elle let out a cry, falling to her knees. The door slid shut hard and Elle was surrounded by darkness. Shaking and frightened, Elle tried to gather her bearings, searching frantically for something to grip on.

A flare of light to her right made her gasp and recoil. When she looked she noticed that a strong fire began to burn within a fireplace, and just feet away stood Malik's towering figure.

"Take off your clothes."

He ordered coldly, his eyes dragging down over her figure with intent. Elle was taken aback.

"What?"

She gasped, unsure that she heard him right.

"Your clothes, woman. Take them off."

He insisted.

Elle pushed herself up to her feet, arms tightening around her chest as she stared at him in fear.

"Why—what are you doing? Please, just talk to me."

"I have no reason to say anything to you, and you have no right to address me in that way." He hissed, taking an advancing step toward her.

Elle took a step back, fear choking her chest.

"I am the Sheikh, and when I order you to remove your clothes, you will obey me."

"What's the matter with you? Why are you behaving like this?"

Malik took another step toward her, his hand shooting out to grab her around her robe. Elle let out a scream when he yanked her toward the fireplace, tripping her over the rug.

Her back collided roughly with the ground, forcing her breath out of her chest. Malik loomed over her and through the color of the flames she could see the intent burn like lust in his eyes.

"You speak to me like I am supposed to care, silly woman."

Tears burned in her eyes as she tried to push him away.

"Zayn, stop, please! Please."

Something slapped against her cheek, forcing her head in the other direction. Pain exploded through her head, made white stars shoot around her vision as her world tipped.

She could feel his hands yanking at the fabric of her bathrobe, and she tried weakly to push him off.

"I thought I told you to never call me that." He snarled against her neck, and she could feel his mouth on her skin, biting and sucking roughly without holding back.

A sharp groan of pain escaped her throat, her hand began to reach for something—anything—to get him off.

To her immense relief, she found the slim handle of an iron poker, and without another thought Elle swung it hard against Malik's head. It collided roughly, and he broke away with a shout.

She was on her feet just a moment later, swinging the poker wildly at this man even as she tried to hold back sobs of fear and torment.

"Stay away from me!"

"You stupid bitch!" Malik snarled, lunging for her.

Elle swung the poker again, the tip slashing against Malik's cheek and ripping a dark wound down his face. He let out another shout, sounding wild in his anger.

"I will show you what happens when you disobey me!"

Suddenly, his body doubled over, and Elle gasped. Muscles rippled and expanded, his body becoming large and immense. The change made Elle stare in horror, watching in shock as the man—now beast—writhed, face elongating into a snout with fangs and long tongue. Elle let out a high pitched scream when the creature faced her with violent eyes.

"You will *never* escape!"

It spoke, rough and animalistic and Elle felt her body backpedal for her life.

"*Malik, no!!*" Elle shrieked.

"ELLE!!"

The door behind her slammed open. Elle whirled around, eyes wide when she saw a far too familiar face.

Malik stood at the doorway, gasping and staring at her with wild concern. Mind spinning, Elle nearly collapsed.

Malik...? What?

"Elle, get away from him!" Malik shouted, rushing further inside the cabin toward her. Elle lifted her hands, not wanting him to approach her.

Instead, Elle darted toward the farthest wall, wanting to avoid both this beast and the man whose face she had believed had transformed.

The beast let out a low rumble, like a laugh before shifting down to its four paws. *A bear...* Elle thought vacantly as she stared in shock, body shaking in fright.

"*Well, now, it's been a while, brother.*" The beast spoke, deep guttural sounds that made each word grating to her ears.

Malik stood before the Bear, holding his ground and glaring hatefully into the beast's eyes.

"Kamal," Malik spat.

"How dare you attempt to take Elle from me?"

"An eye for an eye, is that not what we've learned?"

The bear replied, taking several long strides around the cabin, never breaking the stare down with the man.

Elle watched the exchange with growing confusion, unsure how to handle this chain of events.

"You've taken everything I ever wanted. Now I take the woman you now desire. Is that not fair?"

"No one's taken anything from anyone," Malik replied icily.

"As the eldest, the inheritance is rightfully mine."

"*LIAR!*" The bear roared. Elle slapped her hands to her ears, sinking against the wall to avoid being seen. "

You told me you never wanted the empire! You promised me that I would be the one to take your place as heir!"

Malik was unperturbed.

"Things change, Kamal. I stopped running away years ago. It's time you end this idiot crusade of yours and return home."

"And then what?" The Bear let out another laugh, vicious and awful.

"To await banishment? We both know father has been searching for an excuse to rid himself of his youngest son. Too much of an embarrassment to the empire, too much of a burden."

Malik's expression changed to a pained look, "You know that is not true. Father loves you, Kamal."

"Hilarious to hear that from the favorite!" The animal roared.

"Never has he been able to tell us apart, until now! But now that I have my chance, I can get rid of you and gain everything you have. Luck is on my side tonight, brother."

And suddenly, the bear lunged toward Malik, pouncing with such force that they both tumbled out and through the door. The wood splintered hard from the collision.

Elle let out another shriek, watching wildly as man and bear began to wrestle.

Running outside, she watched as the bear tried to bite down on Malik's neck. Instead, the dark-skinned man threw an arm up, gritting his teeth when his brother's jaws clamped down over the flesh of his arm. Blood exploded from the wounds, dripping over Malik's face and staining his clothes.

Elle gasped, throwing a hand to her mouth as she watched the fight proceed. Malik lifted his legs before kicking hard at the bear's stomach, throwing the beast over his head.

The bear rolled, claws swiping hard in the direction of the man, managing to slash at Malik's chest.

Four long stripes over his chest burst with crimson and in the darkness of night, Elle could see him double over for a moment, grasping to the wounds.

"Zayn!" Elle shouted.

"Stay back!" He snapped back, throwing his wounded arm in her direction.

And then his body was suddenly writhing as well. *"Priya! Take her away!"*

Without warning, a small petite figure darted in front of Elle, making the woman yelp in surprise.

Priya's eyes were wild with focus, grabbing around Elle's wrists before pulling her.

"Look at me, *gori*. Are you wounded?"

Elle couldn't reply, her eyes jumping back to Malik's figure, unable to tear her attention away as Malik's body expanded not unlike she had seen the other Malik's body do. A loud roar escaped Malik's throat, filling the air with its resonance.

"*Gori!*" Priya exclaimed, yanking at Elle's face to look at her. "Stop looking and come with me. We need to get you away from him."

"But—Malik… What—" Elle stammered, but Priya didn't give her a chance to protest, pulling the woman with her with surprising force.

Still, Elle turned her head to try to see, her eyes wide as she beheld the two beasts collide with thunderous power.

Claws swiped left and right, and in the scramble, Elle could no longer tell who her Malik was and who was the imposter.

Priya yanked her away from the battle towards Malik's Mercedes Benz, stopping short when one of the bears let out a particular high roar. Turning her head in the direction of the battle, the woman gave a sound of distress before turning toward Elle.

"You get in the car and you drive away, do you understand me? Get out of here and you don't come back."

"Priya—what is happening?" Elle asked gripping to the woman's hands tightly.

"What is he—who was that other man?"

"Just *go, gori!*" Priya snapped before tearing herself away and rushing toward the sounds of the battle.

The last thing Elle saw of the woman was her body shift as well before disappearing into the woods. But Elle couldn't just leave. She just couldn't.

Another roar burned through the air and Elle felt her stomach fall.

Zayn…

Running back toward where Priya had disappeared, Elle tried to focus on the task at hand, but her body was shaking so hard and stumbling over tree roots nearly made Elle collapse against the earth.

But she pushed onward; she needed to know that Malik was alright.

The firelight from within the cabin was the only thing that cast a light over the area, shining over three bears as they roared and attacked each other. Elle paused to watch, the cold air stinging against her throat.

One of the larger bears was rearing, pushing its weight over its hind legs before slamming down over the earth. The other two bears pulled away from the attack, and Elle noticed one of them—a smaller built bear—dart to the side and lunge toward the bear's head, jaws snapping hard against its neck.

The third bear was pouncing once more, slashing its claws at the other bears chest. The first bear let out a snarl, slapping its immense paw against the smaller bear and shoving it away.

The smaller bear bounced off the earth before turning to its feet, snarling viciously through a parted maw.

The two large bears faced off, rising to their hind legs and shoving at each other, enraged roars echoing through the woods and making Elle brace herself against the nearest tree.

She had no idea what to think, no idea what to do, until one of the bears slammed into the other, forcing the animal on its back. Its jaw was instantly on the other's neck, aiming to kill. The smallest bear tackled the big bear away, and the two spun and tumbled over the earth.

The other bear turned, letting out pained grunts, one of its legs was bleeding, dragging dark trails of crimson. Elle remembered how Malik had been biting in that same arm, and gasped when she saw the bear stumble.

The small bear must be Priya.

Finally gathering her bearings, Elle tried to figure out what to do, but she could only sit back and watch as the bears battled it out.

It seemed to go on for forever until the smaller bear was suddenly thrown against a tree. A sharp whine escaped through its throat and the sound revived the bear that Elle knew to be her Malik.

It whirled and attacked the opposing beast that towered over Priya's still body. Elle felt a gasp lodge in her throat.

Priya... no...!

Hurrying, Elle ran around the zone of battle, hoping to reach the small bear. When she arrived, Priya's body had already shifted back to its familiar petite and very human form.

Haggard breaths escaped the woman's body and Elle was happy at least to note she was still alive, but wounded. Gingerly, Elle grabbed the woman's body, pulling her from the battle with some effort. Priya may have been small, but she wasn't very light. Falling to her knees, Elle pulled the woman close against her chest, her eyes jumping toward the battle.

One of the bears made a last tackle, throwing the other against the cabin walls. The wood split with a mighty crack.

The bear let out a last snarl, pushing itself back up to its paws amongst the rubble. It began to scramble away, but was stopped when the roof of the cabin shuddered and snapped, caving over the bear's head and swallowing it whole.

Elle let out a cry, hoping that that hadn't been her Malik. The lone bear watched the cabin collapse, haggard breaths escaping it as the last of the rubble settled into silence.

Darkness found its way around them once more and when Elle's eyes adjusted, she could see the bear begin to shift and groan.

The large figure dwindled back into a familiar body, yet Elle dared not make a move, gripping to Priya's unconscious frame tightly.

Finally, she saw dark liquid drip from his arm into the earth, and the sight alone made her gasp out in relief, before she was shouting.

"Zayn!" She called, and she saw him turn around.

"Elle…?" He called back, before he stumbled and fell.

Elle cried out when he fell over the earth. Placing Priya back over the ground, Elle hurried toward where Malik had fallen.

She reached around him, tried to help him stand from his knees.

"Are you hurt? How bad is it?" Elle asked, her hands shaking as she searched his body for more wounds.

"I'll…I'll be alright," Malik said gently, before looking up at her.

"Are you alright? He didn't hurt you, did he?"

Elle shook her head.

"I'm fine. But we need to get you out of here."

"Where's Priya?" Malik asked, suddenly sounding desperate to find the other woman.

"I'm alive," Elle heard and when they turned around, Priya was standing just feet away, holding a hand to her ribs.

"She's right, Zayn… we need to go."

"Right." Malik said, before turning his attention back in the direction of the fallen cabin.

"Kamal…" Priya spoke, voice sounding small. "Is he…?"

Malik turned away, pushing himself up to his feet with the help of Elle.

When he spoke, his voice was small and pain filled. "Let's go home."

The walk toward the car was strenuous as both Priya and Malik were injured, and despite Elle's insistence, Priya took the wheel and drove them far away from the cabin.

The drive back was silent and heavy and for that entire time Elle could only stare out the window at the sky above before the gentle hum of the engine lulled her to an uneasy sleep.

Chapter 17

Three days later

"The matter is settled," Priya's voice was strong with conviction, her hazel eyes staring into the digital eyes of impressive figures of state.

One of them, was covered in special robes that signified his alliance to the Malik family, and his eyes narrowed at Priya's announcement.

"Sheikh Zayn Abd al Malik is no longer in danger. His brother, Kamal Abd al Malik has been disposed of. So the biggest threat to the heir and the empire is no longer around to cause any more issues."

"You are certain Kamal is truly gone?"

One of the men questioned in Arabic, looking uncertain.

"Please pardon our incredulity, Sheikha Priya Abdul al Hamik," another man said this time in English.

"But this is not the first time Kamal has disappeared only to reappear to cause more havoc."

"I can assure you," Priya spoke, eyes flashing.

"Kamal is dead. Zayn himself slew him."

A series of gasps followed at Priya's revelation.

"If the council is pleased, then I must be excused. I must go see to the Sheikh's well being."

"He was wounded in the battle?"

"Yes, but it was nothing he cannot handle, Respected Sirs. I have already spoken to the Sheikh's father, and he has been made aware of the matter."

"What of the *gori*?" The first questioned.

"Can we be certain she can be trusted?"

At this, Priya smiled.

"There are few people here that I can trust with the Sheikh's life, Master Mualim. Elle Roberts, surprisingly, has certainly proven herself to be one of them."

Chapter 18

When Elle woke, she found herself over a large and comfortable bed, covered in a thin nightgown and fresh linens for sheets. It took her a moment for her to reorient herself when she spotted the tall figure standing feet away from the bed and staring out a long glass door.

A black robe settled over his shoulders, and in the dying light of day, the last of the sun's rays curled over his figure like something out of a fairytale.

Elle sat up on the bed, not entirely sure how she got there.

"Zayn…?"

He gave a small start before turning to face her, his dark eyes now a piercing amber beneath the sunlight.

"Forgive me, did I wake you?"

Elle shook her head, frowning slightly.

"How did I get here?"

Malik smiled at her as he turned and approached her. The black robe fell over his chest, not covering much of his torso and exposing his powerful figure.

Her eyes fell over the ripples of flesh, remembering heatedly how that same body had pressed itself against hers in hard passionate friction.

"You fell asleep outside my waiting room," Malik explained.

"So I had a couple of servants bring you here."

The reminder of the battle made her rise to her feet, her eyes searching for signs of the wounds that Kamal had placed over his body. Instead, her eyes found none, surprising her.

She approached Malik, her hands reaching the skin of his torso worriedly. He remained still for her, watching her with a warm gaze as she trailed her fingertips over his skin.

"You were injured," Elle said, meeting his eyes with a searching expression.

"I remember you being injured."

"I was." Malik said, nodding before lifting his hands to take hers.

"But… as you can remember, I'm not exactly a regular person."

Elle glanced away, recounting her last conversation with Priya when they had arrived.

Elle had been treated for a bruise over her face and a few cuts on her body, and she was curious that they hadn't been taken to a hospital. Priya soon appeared to explain that they had their own team of physicians and that Malik would be taken care of.

"You remember everything, do you not?" Priya had questioned, hazel eyes digging into her own.

Elle had nodded solemnly.

"Yes. Could…could you tell me what is going on?"

To her surprise, Priya gave her a nod before taking a seat ahead of her.

"The first thing you need to know is that we are not the only ones of our kind in this world."

"Priya told me of what you are," Elle said after a moment, swallowing slowly.

"That you are known as Shifters."

"That is correct." Malik said.

Elle peered up into his eyes, taking in the curve of his jaw, the curl of his dark hair that teased his dark eyes.

"You are not a monster," she said, but it wasn't a question.

She was affirming something within herself, and Malik's expression tightened somewhat.

"In a manner of speaking." He said.

Elle shook her head, lifting one of her hands from his hold to gingerly place over his cheek.

For three days, she had been torn between a myriad of emotions. Anger, betrayal, confusion, heart-break, misunderstanding…

She had been furious over everything that had happened, and so she had been unable to do much aside from sitting down and listening to Priya's explanation. For hours, Elle had contemplated through everything, had cried tears of such torn pain that she had half a mind to turn and run away.

But she couldn't run away. She couldn't hide anymore.

She would not hide from him.

Elle may not know much, she may not understand any of this, but in the time she had spent together with Malik, she felt like she had gotten to know him fairly well.

Even though all of this threw her for such a tailspin, now that she stood before this man and stared into his eyes, she wondered why she had doubted him so much these past couple of days.

"You may be an absolute and arrogant bastard, Zayn Abd al Malik," she said, pronouncing his name with the same trill Priya had taught her.

He raised his brows at her words, but then she smiled, "You may be an infuriating idiot, but… you are not a monster."

His eyes widened, lips parting for a disbelieving sigh to escape past his teeth.

Elle's smile widened, she was probably in over her head, but she knew that there was no going back now. She didn't want to go back anymore.

Reaching up, she pressed her lips to his in a soft kiss, one he returned with some caution. When she pulled away, she sensed a question in his eyes.

"Does this mean you have a crush on me, Miss Roberts?"

He asked and he was back to being the same Malik she had met and found herself falling for.

Rolling her eyes, Elle brought him back down to kiss her once more.

"Just kiss me, you moron." She muttered against his mouth.

He chuckled against her mouth, but at her words, he suddenly dipped down to sweep her into his arms, yanking her body firmly against his.

Elle gasped against him, feeling their hips rub delightfully with the motion. Malik walked ahead, leading her blindly towards the bed in the large room.

When they collapsed against the covers, Elle let out a soft moan when she felt his hands run down her sides to hitch her legs over his hips, rubbing a clothed erection against her dampening heat.

She ran her fingernails up and down his back, peeling off the linen robe from his skin to expose him to her.

Malik followed suit, finding the hem of her nightgown before pushing the thin fabric up over her hips to expose her bare flesh to the cool air around them.

She felt her nipple harden in anticipation, her body shaking as he dipped down to worship gentle kisses over her neck and collarbone, paying special attention to the bruises Kamal had caused.

"I should've been there sooner," Malik said, pausing to look down at her flesh with something akin to regret.

"You saved me," Elle replied, fixing him with a reassuring smile.

"That's all that matters."

He bent down to press another warm kiss to her lips, drawing out pleasant moans from her throat as his fingers burned trails of pleasure down her skin before finding the swell of her breasts.

Elle arched her back into his touch, gasping a deep moan as she felt lust swirl within her blood and make her grind harder against his hips.

Malik ducked down, dragging his lips over the sensitive flesh of her chest.

"I want you, Elle…" Malik groaned, bucking against her hips and drawing out sweet moans from her throat.

"I want you."

"I want you too," Elle said, her body heating up with the need to connect them together again.

Malik pulled away, dragging himself down to her belly and lacing kiss after kiss against her skin.

Elle dragged her hands into his hair, pulling gently at the roots as she continued to buck against him.

In sheer moments, Malik had placed himself between her legs, his hot breath sending shivers through her body.

He pulled off her panties, sliding the material with such erotic slowness, Elle was certain to come apart if he didn't touch her.

Her pleas were met by several kisses he placed against her trembling thighs. He disappeared from her vision the second she felt his tongue drag up her folds, Elle's back arching tight like a strung bow.

His tongue flicked against her, making her see stars and pull her towards a careening climax.

Before she could attempt to stop him, her body began to twitch, her breath hitching high in a moan against the roof of her mouth.

Stars erupted in her blood, making her feel like she had been launched into outer space, surrounded by glorious sights and sensations that for a sure moment, Elle forgot her own name.

He pulled away after a moment of licking up her juices, and Elle lazily searched for him as her body rested from being yanked so thoroughly through a river of desire.

When he appeared back over her, he was grinning down at her, satisfied with her half-lidded expression and languid blinks.

"You alright there, *habibi*?"

"Hmm," Elle mumbled back, "Is… is that all you got?"

He laughed again, dipping down to press a loving kiss against the corner of her mouth.

"Not to worry, *habibi*. I came prepared this time."

Gently, she felt him lift her legs, noticing that he had settled a pillow beneath her lower back before he settled himself between her.

Both her legs rested against his shoulders and Elle couldn't help but be grateful she took yoga for her P.E credit back in high school.

Malik pressed both of his hands on the back of her thighs, and she felt a familiar length rub against her core.

She let out a slow sigh, enjoying the sensation on her sensitive flesh.

"You feel amazing, Elle," Malik said softly, and when she looked at him, she could see that familiar expression of profound pleasure make his face slacken delightfully.

"I hope you're a little more ready for me this time."

Elle nodded at him, her hands reaching up to grip to his biceps, the muscles curling tight beneath her fingertips.

"Make me feel good, Zayn."

"My pleasure," Malik said gently before aligning himself against her entrance.

He wasted no time before he was pushing into her, and the sensation of being filled once more by him made her feel so warm and content. It was a feeling of completion she hadn't felt before and wondered how she had managed to find happiness without him now.

Slowly, he pumped into her, humming to himself when her walls fluttered around him, getting used to his size.

"Delicious," he breathed, retracting his hips before pushing back into her.

Elle moaned, her legs tightening over his shoulders as he positioned himself back and forth against her.

He kept a steady pace, easing Elle down another orgasm that came around her like a warm hug. She came quietly this way, her lips parted wide to release a silent scream of satisfaction.

She wasn't completely done with her orgasm, her walls clenching and shivering around his length when he pulled back and slammed back into her with newfound zeal.

Elle let out a scream, eyes popping open at the sensation, before she let out another gasp. Their breaths intermingled as he leaned forward, pounding into her and watching her body bounce with every slap of their hips.

"Z-Zayn, Zayn!" Elle screamed, her body spasming with every perfect thrust of his narrow hips.

Malik groaned in reply, sliding one of her legs off of his shoulder to shift her hips and provide them a different angle.

The change suddenly made him strike against a particular spot within Elle that made her let out a shriek, so loud that Zayn even threw a hand to cover against her lips.

"Too loud—*pant pant*—you'll alert the entire city!"

He exclaimed but there was a wicked grin over his mouth and Elle was too far gone in sensations to care.

"*There, right there!*" She shouted against his palm, "*Don't stop!*"

Zayn wasted no more time, bucking hard against her and hitting her in that amazing place again and again, making Elle snap and turn with each earth shattering blow.

Sure enough, he was groaning against her, taking her leg over his head to slide behind her, his strong arm holding onto her leg as he proceeded to drill into Elle so thoroughly she was practically sobbing with satisfaction.

Eventually, it was far too much for both of them to carry on for much longer before Zayn was hitting his climax, bending down to dig his teeth against her neck as Elle let out another high pitched cry.

One of his hands gripped to her breast, massaging the globe of flesh with frantic touches and nearly overwhelming Elle completely.

He shuddered against her, his dick throbbing furiously inside her as her walls clamped down and milked and wrenched his orgasm from him.

When they both collapsed against the mattress, sweat soaked and gasping for air, Elle couldn't help but allow her mind to fade away into a white field of bliss.

"Elle," she heard Malik hum behind her.

"You're a beautiful dream, Elle… and you're all mine."

His words made her heart soar, made her grin and make her feel incredibly confident, made her feel like she was the most beautiful woman in the world.

Turning around, she placed a sloppy kiss against his lips, giggling airily.

"Not quite," she said and when he blinked at her in surprise, she gave him a sultry smile.

"I can't make it that easy for you, your Excellency."

"Oh?"

He asked, returning her smile with equal deviant luster.

"And what do you have in mind?"

"Let's just say I have my own set of Rules that you must obey. That won't be a problem will it?"

Malik laughed, "You've accepted me in every shape and form, my love. It's not a problem at all."

Elle smiled before sinking deep into his arms.

"Good luck, your excellency," she said, echoing the words he gave her on the day they met.

"You're going to need it."

--

End

PREVIEW OF 'CHOSEN BY HER BEAR' BY ASHLEY HUNTER

I.

Why oh why didn't you, Ava Williams, look that boy in the eye, you stupid girl.

I had to mentally chide myself every time after such an episode (one would think that I would get used to it by now, but no).

What would be that librarian thinking about right now? *Probably not me.*

For a bright few moments, he and I were the only two souls in the universe; that is until the stupid woman behind me suddenly decided that she was running late for her weekly Wednesday gym class or something. I would have argued had I not been myself in need of a gym class. *Sigh.*

Anyway, this has been my problem as far back as I can remember. Not born with superhuman looks nor inclined to induce anorexia to get a body suitable for a

Victoria's Secret model, I was always on the heavier side and that is where problems started with my love life.

Nonexistent as it is. I recently passed through college without as much as a boyfriend to my name. If my grandmother had to be believed, and it is extremely dubious that she is, *it is your curves, honey.*

I can't bring myself to tell my dear Grammy that it is 2015. But maybe she has a point. What do I know? I am 24 years old and without a lover. There are not many who can boast that. There are not many who would call it boasting.

Ironically enough I have always been confident in my life, knowing what I wanted and who I wanted. It was going after who I wanted that was the difficult part.

My *curves* always made it difficult to maneuver boys like other girls did, wrapping them up around their bony fingers. As for me, I have always been crippled with the fear that nobody would be interested in me, *just because.*

In principle I knew that the world should be a judgment free zone and I should embrace who I am, but damned if the real world worked like that. Everybody likes to dole out principles and paste them on their cars as bumper sticks; living them, that's a whole different ball game.

No matter what everybody said, which ranged from *looks don't matter* to *find someone who loves you for your mind, and not your body,* I had never been able to get the confidence to move beyond a certain wall to reach a point where a guy actually fell for my *brains.*

I know. So very Jane Austen.

Anyhow, this is the sum of it: I am a 24 year old graduate (think of Dustin Hoffman, only female and thirty pounds heavier. OK, don't think of Dustin Hoffman), no men in sight and the weight of loneliness on my still young shoulders, pressing me down.

Couldn't a knight in shining armor come along? *I shouldn't think like that. Women don't need knights anymore.* But I need a relationship. No, not need. I *want* a relationship. Is it too much to ask? Does pining for it make me a villain for my gender? Where's my John Wayne or Humphrey Bogart? Hell, where's my Raylan Givens?

Maybe I should not be thinking about fictional characters.

Reality is stranger than fiction and I had always lived by that rule. But nothing in my life had happened that proved this axiom. That didn't stop me from believing in it, but I had to agree that the strength of my conviction was waning, as is if often the case when you keep waiting for moments that never come.

What happened in the next few weeks is beyond strange. I should never have doubted it.

This is the story of what happened.

II.

The Beginning

It was a dark and rainy night. *It really was, I am not stating a cliché of noirs. Thor must be having one hell of a party.*

I had been held back at my office due to a sudden crisis in the Middle East. I worked for a political think tank and due to the uncertain global condition; our work hours usually didn't limit themselves to Pacific Standard Time.

I had my umbrella open but it wasn't doing much good. The rain seemed to be coming in from all four directions; the wind sure wasn't helping. There were no taxis to be found and it wasn't a surprise.

Who would be willing to risk driving in weather like this? I kept on walking, the cold biting my skin like a sharp teethed animal. The thought of finally reaching home, in my warm cozy bed was all that kept me going. *If only I had somebody to cozy up to. Hmmm. Wouldn't that be nice?*

I mentally shook myself. This wasn't the time or the place to think about such thing; though I couldn't help but playback the lyrics of the famous song in me: *Let me kiss you hard in the pouring rain.* Truer words had rarely been said.

Maybe this was the reason or maybe it was the water pummeling the leaves of the trees and the streets and the buildings that I didn't hear anything whistle by near me.

If it had been a quite night, I surely would have noticed something. But this being the night that it was, I didn't feel someone walk up behind me. I didn't feel when they pressed a cloth over my face, the smell reminding me of hospital rooms and oddly, bars.

Click Here To Read More!

Or Go To: http://amzn.to/1FcPRpl

To Read More Bearilicious Romance By Ashley Hunter, go to: http://amzn.to/1Hpn9Ut

Printed in Great Britain
by Amazon.co.uk, Ltd.,
Marston Gate.